What people have said about *The Land of Roar*:

'A vividly imagined adventure . . . full of heart,
humour and a terrifying villain.'
Fiona Noble, *The Bookseller*

'This is proof, not that it's needed, that Jenny McLachlan is a
writer of enormous heart and versatility. I'm a really big fan.'
Phil Earle

'Roar is an exhilarating, hilarious, vividly drawn tribute to the power of the
childhood imagination, the love of family and the magic we risk losing
as we grow up. If you plan to visit one new place, make it Roar.'
Sarah Driver, author of the Huntress trilogy

'This funny, captivating story is filled with the painful pangs of
growing up and the transporting qualities of imagination.'
Imogen Russell-Williams, *Guardian*

'Finished this truly brilliant book in the wee hours
last night and it's amazing!'
Tamsin Winter, author of *Jemima Small vs the Universe*

'Like *Jumanji* meets Narnia. Pitch perfect balance of funny & creepy!'
Charlotte Lo, author of *We Won an Island*

'Finished this beauty – so much fun and adventure with lovely touches of
humour. A gorgeous story land to escape into – brilliant stuff!'
Vashti Hardy, author of *Wildspark* and the Brightstorm series

'It's so perfect and sad and right. It gave me goosebumps . . .
Great escapist fun and the brother and sister relationship got me
smack bang in the heart. Plus the baddy was super sinister.'
Lindsay Galvin, author of *The Secret Deep*

'I loved The Land of Roar – it was spectacular.'
Sinead O'Hart, author of *The Star-spun Web*

'This book has everything: dragons, danger, disagreeing siblings,
and the most fantastically snooty rocking horse I've ever met.
One of the very best adventures I've been on. Adored it . . . '
Emma Carroll, author of *Secrets of the Sun King* and
When We Were Warriors

The
BATTLE
for
ROAR

JENNY McLACHLAN

First published in Great Britain 2021 by Farshore

An imprint of HarperCollins*Publishers*
1 London Bridge Street, London SE1 9GF

farshore.co.uk

HarperCollins*Publishers*
1st Floor, Watermarque Building,
Ringsend Road, Dublin 4, Ireland

Text copyright © Jenny McLachlan 2021
Illustrations copyright © Ben Mantle 2021
Jenny McLachlan and Ben Mantle have asserted their moral rights.

ISBN 978 1 4052 9814 8
Printed and bound in the UK using 100% renewable electricity
at CPI Group (UK) Ltd
1

Stay safe or ▢ the time
of going ▢ sted by
third pa ▢ ange
an ▢
We ▢ t.

For Julia Churchill, I'm glad you liked this idea.

MITCH

ARCHIE PLAYGO

TANGLED Fo

ROAR

the END →

the CROW'S Nest

Rest

The BAD SIDE

DUNGUN

by ROSE
and ARTHUR

CHAPTER 1

It happens during PE.

We're playing rounders on the field when this huge crow comes flying over the science block. I'm supposed to be bowling, but all I can do is stare up at the sky and watch as the bird flies closer and closer.

'Throw the ball, Trout!' bellows Mr McGill.

My best friend (in the real world), Adam Zeng, waves his bat around. 'Yeah, smash it to me, Arthur. Pretend you're a wizard and that ball is a power crystal that will turn my bones to JELLY!'

Like me, Adam has a big imagination. Unlike me, he sees no reason to hide this fact from the rest of our class. He starts to wobble (like jelly) and laughter breaks out across the field. This enrages Mr McGill, who yells, 'Bowl, Trout, BOWL!'

So I bowl, but just as the ball is leaving my hands the crow dives towards me. I yelp and throw myself to the ground.

'BIRD ATTACK!' screams Adam and the ball smacks into Mr McGill's stomach.

Through my fingers I watch as the bird pecks a crust off the grass, then flies away again.

'That bird was going for you, Arthur,' says Adam as he pulls me to my feet. 'I thought it was going to peck your eyes out!'

'Me too,' I say, glancing nervously at the sky.

Mr McGill isn't amused by the whole crow-ball-in-the-stomach thing. He sends everyone inside to get changed except for me and Adam. Then, with one hand resting protectively on his stomach, he jabs a finger at us and says, 'I want you two jokers to stay out here and pick up litter.'

I look around. Rubbish is scattered across the field. Water bottles and crisp packets drift in the wind. 'What, *all* of it?' I say.

'Yes, Trout, *all* of it,' he says, then he turns and stomps off, calling over his shoulder, 'Useless bowling by the way!'

Once he's out of earshot, Adam squeezes my shoulder

and says, 'Gadzooks, Master McGill is a swine.' Adam's into live-action role play and every weekend he goes to some woods and pretends to be a medieval knight. He doesn't see why he should have to stop just because he's at school and often speaks using ye olde language. I think this is really funny. My sister doesn't.

'Verily 'tis true,' I say – because the medieval thing is addictive and no one is around to hear – and then we start to pick up litter.

After a while Adam says, 'You know what, Arthur? I reckon that crow came from the Land of Roar.'

I freeze, my hand hovering over a sweet wrapper. 'What do you mean?'

'I bet Crowky sent it as a message,' he says, his eyes round with excitement. 'He's basically saying: *Watch out, Arthur Trout, I'm coming to get you!*'

It's hot on the field, boiling, but even so a shiver runs through me. I force myself to laugh. 'Yeah . . . probably!'

'Definitely!' says Adam, then he starts chasing a crisp packet across the field, yelling, 'Come hither, dastardly Monster Munch!'

I have to remind myself that of course Adam is joking and he doesn't believe for one second that Crowky, a wicked scarecrow with wings, is sending me sinister messages via a crow. As far as Adam's concerned, he likes pretending to be a medieval knight, and I like making up stories about a fantasy world called the Land of Roar, and it's one of the

3

reasons we're such good friends. But, as he runs across the field, the cold feeling continues to creep through me. I look up at the sky. The bird has definitely gone, but even so my heart beats fast. Because what Adam doesn't know is that Crowky is one hundred per cent real – from his feathery wings to the tips of his life-sapping fingers – and sending me a creepy message is *exactly* the sort of thing he would do.

CHAPTER 2

After school, Adam and I sit on the wall by the bike shed and wait for my twin sister, Rose, to turn up so we can walk home together. Rose used to hang out with us at school as well, but recently she's become friends with a girl called Kezia and we're seeing less and less of her.

Adam's gutted. He loves everything about Rose – her sarcasm, her fondness for shoving us around, even her ability to beat us in every single running, staring and arm-wrestling match that she forces us to have. I keep telling Adam that if he'd had to share a womb and then most of his life with Rose he wouldn't think she was so great, but he just sighs and says, 'If only!'

While we wait, Adam and I chat about what happened on the field. In our heads the crow has become superhuman in size – as big as an eagle, or, as Adam suggests, a suckling pig. 'You should add it to your story,' he says. 'Now, before you forget what happened.'

I glance around to make sure no one's watching, then get

my notebook out of my bag. It looks like any old notebook but inside I've written down every single thing that's ever happened to me and Rose in Roar. Adam caught me writing in it one day, so I told him it was a story I'd made up. Since then he's always getting me to read it out loud and he knows all about Mitch and Win and the Lost Girls. He even makes suggestions about things I should add 'to make the story better'.

'Say it had "evil eyes",' says Adam as I scribble down a few sentences about the crow, 'and "claws like razor blades"!' Before I can put it away he says, 'Read the start, Arthur, I

love that bit.'

I can never resist talking about Roar so I flick to the front of the notebook, and start to read.

'*Many moons ago, a brother and sister, twin children of a powerful warlock and a wondrous witch, played a game. Using their mighty imaginations they invented a world – Roar – and they filled it with incredible friends including a merwitch called Mitch and a ninja wizard called Win. These magical twins put all the things they loved in the Good Side of Roar, and the things they feared – cats, dead trees, demented scarecrows, their enemy Crowky etc – into the Bad Side. One day, still many moons ago, the twins crawled into an enchanted cave and when they came out of the other side they were in THE LAND OF ROAR. Their imaginations were so powerful their game had come to life!*'

'Awesome,' says Adam, nodding his head appreciatively.

OK, so this isn't *exactly* what happened. Rose and I *are* twins, but Dad isn't a powerful warlock and Mum isn't a wondrous witch. Dad's a postman and Mum's a textiles teacher, but the rest of it is true. Kind of. Our portal to Roar is actually a folding camp bed, but when I told Adam this he said, 'That's rubbish, Arthur. Make it a cave.'

As usual, once I've started talking about Roar I don't want to stop. 'I've done more,' I say. Last night I finished writing down everything that happened during our last visit to Roar. 'Do you want to hear it?'

'Course I do!' says Adam.

'OK, so Crowky's in the sea and Win and Arthur have

just been rescued by the ice dragon, remember?'

Adam nods, then I start reading:

'*Arthur Trout leaped on to the ice dragon's slippery back and dragged Win up next to him. Without stopping to think, he reached out a hand to Crowky. "Come with us!" he demanded.*

'*Crowky's button eyes slid from Arthur to the "NO PROB-LLAMA!" T-shirt floating in the sea. Should he let Arthur Trout, Master of Roar, save his life, or should he try to get the T-shirt? Crowky came to a decision and dived into the freezing waves. His twig fingers wrapped round the T-shirt and a grin spread across his sack face. The T-shirt might be tatty and torn, but Crowky knew it was a magical key that would let him . . .*' I trail off, not sure if I want to read the next bit.

'Go on,' says Adam, nudging me.

'*That would let him escape from Roar and crawl into the real world.*'

Adam snatches the notebook off me and takes over. '*And then Crowky could hunt down Arthur and Rose and their grandad, and stuff them by squeezing the life out of them with his twig fingers!*' Adam cackles with laughter as he grabs my arm and hisses, 'Drain, Arthur, drain!'

'Yep. That's what he'd do,' I say, sweat prickling my skin.

Suddenly a loud voice cries out, 'Arthur, what do you think you're doing?'

I look up to see Rose standing in front of me, arms folded with an angry look on her face.

'Just reading a bit of my story to Adam,' I say.

'Well, I don't think your story sounds very *realistic*, do you?' she says, one eyebrow raised. 'How about you say that Arthur wasn't sitting on the dragon's back but was dangling helplessly from its claws, like *a little mouse*, and that Win was in his *pants*?'

'That would be brilliant!' says Adam. 'And it would be even funnier if Arthur was in his pants too!'

'Good idea,' says Rose, then she spins round and walks towards the gates, calling, 'Hurry up, you two!'

When Rose first found out that I'd read my story to Adam she was furious because we'd agreed never to tell anyone about Roar. But as soon as Adam started talking about her moonlight stallion Prosecco and her deadly dragons she changed her mind.

At school Rose is like any other twelve-year-old, but in Roar she's this incredible creature-tamer who can make dragons roll over for a tummy tickle with one click of her fingers. She loves the fact that someone else finally knows about her skills and agreed that I could keep reading my story to Adam as long as I never let him know that Roar is real. Some days this is a really hard promise to keep.

Once we're out of school, Rose looks at us with a sly smile and says, 'So Kezia told me a funny story. Her brother said that two boys in our year freaked out when a crow landed on the field during PE. Apparently one of boys curled up on the floor and started to cry, while the other one ran around the field screaming, "Big one! Big one!"'

'Arthur was *not* crying,' says Adam, outraged. 'He was whimpering, and I was saying, "Begone, begone!"'

'Yeah, and you'd have curled up on the floor if that thing was flying towards you,' I say. 'The crow was massive, Rose!'

She grins. 'I *knew* it had to be you two. So what was it about this bird that scared you so much?'

'It wasn't a *bird*,' scoffs Adam. 'It was one of Crowky's spies delivering a message to Arthur.'

'Oh, yes?' says Rose sarcastically. 'And what was this message?'

'Well, we don't know exactly,' says Adam. 'It was more a general I'm-coming-to-get-you message . . . What I don't get is why Crowky didn't turn up on the playing field himself? He's got the T-shirt, so he could come here if he wanted to, couldn't he? Imagine if he flew down and stuffed Mr McGill. That would be amazing!'

His words make my stomach squirm uncomfortably and I fight the urge to look up at the sky.

'I'll tell you why Crowky didn't turn up himself, Adam,' says Rose. 'Because, just like the Loch Ness Monster, ghosts and your girlfriend in Year Nine, he isn't real.'

Adam gazes at her. 'Gad zooks, you're funny, Rose.'

Rose sucks in her breath. 'Adam, what's the rule about the buffer zone?'

'No medieval stuff within twenty metres of you.'

'That's it,' she says, 'and right now you are less than thirty centimetres away from me.'

'Forgive me, sweetling!'

Rose swings her bag at Adam but he dodges out of the way. So she gets him in a headlock instead. 'Call me "sweetling" again,' she hisses, 'and I'll stop walking home with you.'

'Sorry!' he squeals.

Once Adam has been released we talk a bit more about Roar, then share a packet of Peanut M&Ms while Rose tells us about Kezia's cat. Apparently it's scared of cucumbers and bananas but not courgettes. Soon we reach Adam's road.

He runs towards his house, then, when he's standing outside his gate (and approximately twenty metres away from Rose) he shouts, 'Fare thee well, Lord Arthur and sweet Lady Rose. By my troth 'tis but four days till the summer holidays!' Then he bows, waves an imaginary hat above his head and disappears inside his house.

'Ye gads,' says Rose, unable to help herself, 'I can't believe that boy is one of my best friends.'

We walk on for a moment, then Rose nudges me and grins. 'Just *four days* to go, Arthur. I can't wait!'

She's not talking about the summer holidays but about going back to Roar. On the last day of term Grandad is picking us up from school, taking us to his house and then we're crawling straight through the camp bed and into Roar.

'It's going to be amazing,' I say, and then the two of us are lost in thoughts about Roar. A warm, happy glow surrounds us as we cut across the park, but then I have to go and ruin everything by saying, 'Rose, are you *sure* Crowky didn't send that crow to scare me?'

She bursts out laughing. 'Of course he didn't! Arthur, do you really think that if Crowky wanted to scare you, he'd send a crow to make you bowl badly in rounders?'

'No,' I admit. 'He's more into kidnapping people and setting fire to stuff and destroying lives.'

'Exactly,' she says, giving me a shove. 'Crowky is gone, Arthur, which means this trip to Roar is going to be our best ever!'

CHAPTER 3

There is another reason why this trip to Roar is going to be our best ever: we're going for ten whole days.

When Mum and Dad said they wanted to spend their annual no-twins holiday walking in Spain, Rose and I managed to convince them that one week wasn't nearly enough time to enjoy the Pyrenees and not be with us. Then we went on about how much we loved visiting Grandad, and how it made us feel grown-up and responsible being left on our own, and before we knew it they'd booked a ten-day holiday in Spain.

This meant we could start planning our trip to Roar.

We knew that ten days would give us enough time to do something really special. It was Rose who came up with the idea of an expedition. Along with Win and Mitch, we're going to sail across Roar, further than we've ever been before, to explore the islands that lie beyond The End. They're not frozen and snowy like the rest of The End. They're lush and green and mysterious, and we haven't got a clue what's on them . . . but soon we're going to find out!

The thought of the expedition is so exciting that the last days of school drag by. Rose and I sit through pointless end-of-term lessons, the whole time dreaming about the moment we set sail on our pirate ship, the *Alisha*. If anything, it's even worse at home. Time seems to stand still as we pack bags full of clothes we're never going to wear and listen to Mum and Dad's lectures about looking after Grandad and making sure we get enough fresh air. Ha! If only they knew. Air doesn't get much fresher than when you're flying a dragon over the Bottomless Ocean!

Then, finally, the last day of term arrives.

After breakfast, we say goodbye to Mum and Dad then drag our heavy rucksacks to Langton Academy. Then we have five long lessons to get through. The second the bell rings, Rose and I are shooting out of school with Adam following close behind us.

'What's the big rush?' he says as our rucksacks bang into lockers.

'We don't want to keep Grandad waiting,' Rose calls back.

She needn't have worried. As usual, Grandad is late. Adam stands between us at the side of the road while other children walk home and the buses pull away.

'I'm going to miss you two,' says Adam. 'I asked Mum if you could come camping with us in Wales, but she said there wasn't enough room in our tent.'

Adam can't believe that our mum and dad are going on

holiday without us, even though we keep telling him we don't mind. 'Honestly, we're fine,' I say. 'We love it at Grandad's.'

'I know,' he says, 'but, Arthur, the campsite's got *alpacas!*'

Rose hides a smile. Like me, she must be thinking about all the merfolk, unicorns and dragons that are waiting for us in Roar.

'Where's Grandad?' I say, peering down the road. Although I'm desperate to get to Roar, I don't mind him being a bit late because he's got a very embarrassing car. He's attached so many bits to it from other cars that it looks like it belongs to a clown.

'There he is!' says Rose.

His car comes rattling down the road followed by a huge cloud of smoke. Grandad hits the brakes then toots his horn three times, just in case we haven't spotted him . . . parked in front of us . . . in his clown car.

He leans out of the window and gives us a massive smile. His hair and beard are fluffier than ever and they stand out against his dark brown skin. 'Well, what are you waiting for?' he says. 'Get in!' I'm about to throw my bag in the boot, when he says, 'Boot's broken, Arthur. I'm going to find a new one at the scrapyard tomorrow.'

Of course he is.

Before we can leave Adam has to have some medieval banter with Grandad, and then he bids us a long 'adieu'. This involves him doing a deep bow and then saying to Rose, 'Fair thee well, Rose, my lambkin!'

15

'I'll *never* be your lambkin, Adam,' she says, winding up her window before he can attempt to kiss her hand. Grandad pulls away from the kerb with a few more loud blasts on his horn.

'This is it,' says Grandad, as we leave school and a waving Adam behind us. 'This is IT, twins! The big one . . . the expedition to beyond The End!' I think Grandad might be even more excited than we are.

Rose tuts. 'Grandad, concentrate on the road.'

'I always concentrate on the road,' he says, bending down to fiddle with the stereo. Suddenly Katy Perry's *Roar* blasts out of the speakers. 'I thought this might get you in the mood!'

As the music thuds out we drive down winding country roads and I let myself think about Roar. This isn't our first trip back since we left Crowky in the sea. We've actually had three minibreaks, one or two nights when Mum and Dad let us stay over at Grandad's and we managed to crawl through the camp bed. These were fun but nowhere near long enough. We only had time to hang out with Mitch and Win, have a quick fly on the dragons and do some expedition planning.

Once we even managed to pop to Roar for an hour after Grandad made a big Sunday lunch and Mum and Dad fell asleep watching *Escape to the Country*. It was risky but worth it. When they called up the stairs to tell us it was time to go, we were just tumbling out of the camp bed, breathless from the dragon race we'd had over the Tangled Forest.

But the very best thing about these visits to Roar is that we haven't seen or heard from Crowky. It's like he's vanished. Still, no one is letting their guard down. Mitch, Stella and Win all know that he's got the T-shirt and the power that this gives him. They also know that – like any object from home – he can use the T-shirt to get through the tunnel and get to us, and they're doing everything they can to protect us. Mitch has got her merfolk friends patrolling the seas, and the Lost Girls have been camping out across Roar, searching for any sign of Crowky. Win's done his bit too. He's put so many booby traps around the On-Off Waterfall that getting in and out of Roar is quite hazardous.

The cool breeze from the open window blows on my face and the happy feeling comes back. Soon I'm going to be flying a dragon through air peppered with sparks from the dragon's fiery breath. The happiness grows until my whole body is tingling. We don't know where Crowky is, but if he comes back, we're ready for him!

A strange sound pulls me out of my thoughts and back to the car. I can hear singing . . . and it's coming from the boot. 'What's that?' I say, wondering if Grandad's fixed up an extra speaker in there.

'What's what?' Grandad turns off the stereo, and, just for a second, the singing continues.

'*That*,' I say.

'Ah,' says Grandad, chuckling. 'That's my little surprise.

Take a look.'

I peer over the back seat and into the boot. There's a blanket in there covering something bumpy.

'What is it, Arthur?' says Rose.

I pull back the blanket, and what I see makes me scream so loud Grandad hits the brakes. Grinning up at me is Wininja: my best wizard-ninja friend in the world.

'SURPRISE!' he yells, leaping up and throwing his arms round me.

CHAPTER 4

I stare at Win. I can hardly believe that he is here, in the real world, sitting in my grandad's boot! It's too incredible for my eyes to take in, not to mention totally illegal.

'Hi, Arthur,' Win says. 'Hi, Rose!'

Rose blinks, mouth hanging open, then shouts, 'Grandad! What were you thinking?'

While Rose tells Grandad off, I continue staring at Win. 'How did you even get here?' I say.

'Well, your grandad has got this key, and he used it to open this door thingy, and then I climbed in. It was really easy.'

'No, not into the boot,' I say, 'into this world, *Home*. Win, you're not supposed to have a single thing that belongs to us.'

'Oh, you left this behind the last time you came.' And from his robes he pulls out a Mint Imperial.

He must have got it when we visited after the massive Sunday lunch; Grandad always gives us a Mint Imperial after a family meal and we went to Roar on the spur of the moment. We didn't plan it, and I obviously didn't empty my pockets like I usually do.

'But . . . I'd *never* leave something from Home in Roar,' I say.

'Maybe it fell out of your pocket?' says Win.

'Or maybe you put your hand into my pocket when we were flying Vlad over the Tangled Forest and took it out.'

He grins. 'Yeah, that's what I did!'

'Win, you know the rules.'

'I know and at first I was just going to eat it, honestly. I licked it, like, a hundred times, but then I thought I should keep it for emergencies, like now.'

'So what was the big emergency?'

'I really, really, REALLY wanted to see you!' he says, then he's throwing his arms round me again and he's so happy it's impossible for me to stay angry with him.

'Win, get out of the boot and put on a seat belt,' says Rose.

'What's a seat belt?' he says as he scrambles into the backseat and sits next to me. This is the first of many questions Win asks as we drive on towards Grandad's town.

'What are *they*, Arthur?'

'Cows.'

'*Cows* . . .' he says, his voice filled with wonder, followed by. 'And what's that?'

'A burger van.'

'A *burger van* . . . What's a burger?'

And so on until we reach Grandad's house. It's a relief to be bumping down his driveway knowing we're safely hidden from view by the overgrown trees.

'Park down the side of the house, Grandad,' says Rose. 'We don't want Mazen to see Win.'

'What's Mazen?' says Win.

'A horrible girl with a trampoline,' I say.

'I know what a trampoline is!' he says triumphantly.

Grandad turns off the engine and there's a moment of silence before he says, 'Next stop, Roar!' Then Rose puts on Katy Perry again and we're all singing along at the tops of our voices, high on the excitement of what's about to happen, and Win's singing the loudest.

'Hang on,' I say, shouting to be heard over the others. 'How come Win knows all the words?'

CHAPTER 5

It turns out this isn't Win's first trip to Home. This becomes clear when he expertly makes us all cheese toasties and uses my grandad's first name. 'Pickle, Jay?' he asks as he peers into the fridge.

'Yes, please,' says Grandad. 'A smidgen of pineapple. You know how I like it.'

Win and Grandad admit that Win has visited a few times over the past month, usually on a Saturday. 'I didn't see the harm,' says Grandad. 'We just have a curry and watch a bit of *Ninja Warrior*, that's all.'

'Beat the wall! Beat the wall! BEAT THE WALL!' chants Win.

I stare at him. 'Win, I don't know what you're talking about, and this is *my* world.'

It's a bit disturbing to discover that Win knows exactly how Grandad takes his tea and how to sort the recycling, but Rose and I are so keen to get to Roar that we haven't got time to tell Grandad off.

'He won't do it again,' promises Grandad. 'We'll eat these toasties, then Win will eat the Mint Imperial, and there will be no more visits to Home.'

Reluctantly Win agrees.

'Now where's my pineapple pickle?' says Grandad.

'We've run out,' says Win. 'I'll pop down to the cellar and get some.'

'I'll go,' I say quickly. Rose and I aren't the only ones in this family with a secret world. Grandad has always said that he's got a world like Roar hidden inside a jam cupboard in his cellar. We've never seen this world, but Grandad's told us enough stories about it to make me think Win shouldn't go anywhere near that cupboard. I can just imagine him crawling inside and then me and Rose having to go and rescue him.

'Arthur,' says Rose as I leave the kitchen, 'if we're going to get to Roar before sunset, we need to get going. Don't do anything silly down there.'

'I won't,' I say as I open the door to the cellar.

I press the light switch and somewhere below me a bare bulb flickers into life. I walk down, breathing in the familiar cellar smell of damp and wood shavings. The banister creaks and my heart speeds up. This is actually the first time I've been down here since Grandad told me about what was inside his jam cupboard. Really I should be desperate to see another world like Roar, but something has always stopped me from coming down these stairs.

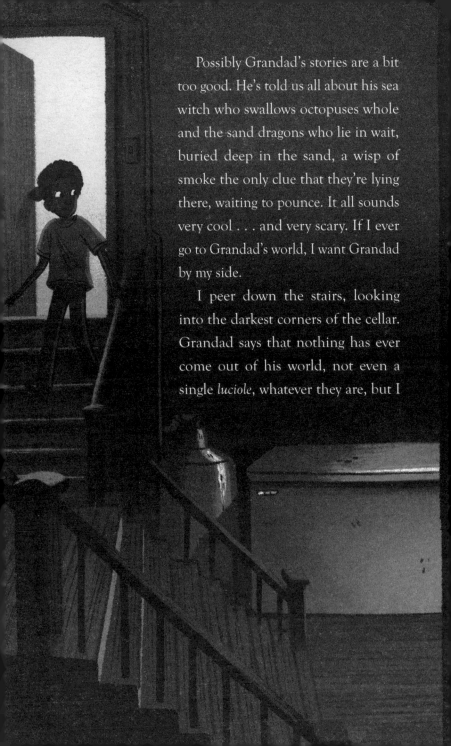

Possibly Grandad's stories are a bit too good. He's told us all about his sea witch who swallows octopuses whole and the sand dragons who lie in wait, buried deep in the sand, a wisp of smoke the only clue that they're lying there, waiting to pounce. It all sounds very cool . . . and very scary. If I ever go to Grandad's world, I want Grandad by my side.

I peer down the stairs, looking into the darkest corners of the cellar. Grandad says that nothing has ever come out of his world, not even a single *luciole*, whatever they are, but I

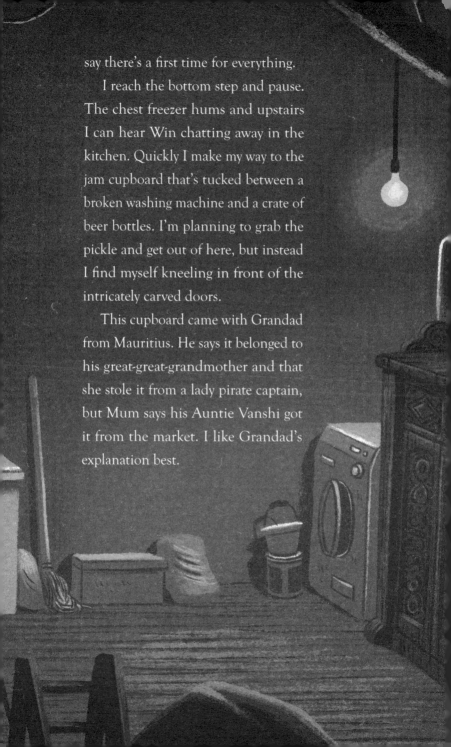

say there's a first time for everything.

I reach the bottom step and pause. The chest freezer hums and upstairs I can hear Win chatting away in the kitchen. Quickly I make my way to the jam cupboard that's tucked between a broken washing machine and a crate of beer bottles. I'm planning to grab the pickle and get out of here, but instead I find myself kneeling in front of the intricately carved doors.

This cupboard came with Grandad from Mauritius. He says it belonged to his great-great-grandmother and that she stole it from a lady pirate captain, but Mum says his Auntie Vanshi got it from the market. I like Grandad's explanation best.

Taking a deep breath, I open the doors.

The cupboard is big and deep and smells of spices, and at the bottom there are rows of dusty jars all labelled with single words: *tamarind, tomato, banana*. The cupboard is big and deep and it smells of spices. When Rose and I asked Grandad if we could visit his world, he just laughed, and said, 'Why not? It's like Roar. If you believe in it, you can get there.' But right now, looking at the solid planks that line the back, it seems impossible that anything could lie beyond them.

I suppose there's one way to find out.

Without stopping to think I push my head into the cupboard until my nose is touching the boards at the back. I stay like this for a few seconds, then a minute. Nothing happens. My first thought is that the magic doesn't work for me, that I don't believe enough, but then another thought creeps into my mind. What if the doorway to Grandad's world is broken? I don't know when Grandad last visited; it could have been months ago. Perhaps he can't go there any more and he doesn't even know . . .

For a few seconds I kneel there with my head shoved deep into the cupboard, wondering what I would do if I ever found out that I couldn't get to Roar. It would be the worst thing that could possibly happen.

Suddenly the cellar light turns off and I'm plunged into darkness. 'Rose?' I shout. 'Win? Is that you?'

Click. Light floods back into the cellar, making me jump.

'Sorry, Arthur!' shouts Grandad. 'I forgot you were down there!'

I grab a jar labelled *pineapple* then take the stairs two at a time.

Grandad is waiting for me in the hallway. 'All right, Arthur?' he says. 'You look a bit pale. You didn't bump into my *sorcière de la mer*, did you?'

I'm not sure what to say, so I decide to go with the truth. 'No, all I saw was a normal old cupboard filled with jam.'

He laughs as he steers me back towards the kitchen. 'Oh, it's old all right, and it is full of jam, but I'd never describe it as *normal*!'

CHAPTER 6

As we eat our toasties Grandad tells us a bit more about his world. 'So you've got Crowky, but I've got Malin. She's a sea witch who lives in a cave, my *sorcière de la mer*, and when she uncoils she can reach the castle in the clouds.'

Win stares at Grandad. 'She sounds *terrible*, Jay. Even worse than Crowky!'

He shrugs. 'Not really. Over the years Malin and I have reached an understanding. As long as I never take any crustaceans out of the sea, she leaves me alone.' Then his eyes light up as he tells us about Malin's wriggling fish earrings and her silver fingertips. He's enjoying himself so much that he starts slipping into French, the language he spoke when he was a boy in Mauritius.

I feel bad listening to him, because I can't help thinking about what happened in the cellar. Of course I could ask when he last visited, but I don't. Grandad looks so happy right now that I don't want to say anything that might bring him down.

'Once,' continues Grandad, 'Malin rescued me from a terrible storm. She simply stood up and I was hoisted to safety on her great pile of hair! Then she strode through the waves as if they were *petites flaques*, you know, puddles!'

I decide I need to push my thoughts about closed doorways out of my head because in a minute we're going up into the attic and I have to believe that the camp bed will take me to Roar, so I look at Grandad and say, 'She sounds amazing.'

Grandad smiles. 'She is, Arthur, she is.'

Win is captivated by everything: Grandad's tales, the cheese oozing from his toastie, and even the chocolate milk that Rose decides to make. 'Whoa . . .' he says as she stirs in the powder. 'Are you using *magic* to do that?'

Win might be loving it here, but my experience in the cellar has only made me more keen to get to Roar. The moment we finish our toasties, I jump up and say, 'Shall we go?'

As usual, we empty our pockets into Grandad's fruit bowl. 'You need to eat that Mint Imperial,' I tell Win, which he does reluctantly.

Then, while Rose puts on her leopard-print onesie, I do my teeth because it's a going-on-a-journey thing to do. Win follows me into the bathroom, eating some toothpaste then flushing the toilet repeatedly. '*Imaginary*,' he whispers as he watches the water swirl around the pan.

Rose sticks her head round the door. 'Ready?' she says.

We follow her up the stairs and slide back the bolts on the attic door. I made Grandad fix these on. If all Win's booby traps fail, and Crowky somehow finds his way into the attic, at least he won't be able to walk straight downstairs. Grandad laughed when I asked him to do this and pointed out that there was a window Crowky could fly out of, but in the end he did it to keep me happy.

Before Rose opens the door, she knocks saying, 'Hello, Crowky, are you in there?' This makes Win cackle with laughter. 'Looks like it's all clear!' she says with a grin.

We step into the attic and I feel the usual rush of happiness. This room is where Rose and I played all the games that brought Roar to life; it's where Rose first wrapped a sleeping bag round her legs, picked up a wand and said, 'I'm a merwitch!' and where a few months ago we pretended the sofa was a boat and then, seconds later, the Bowt appeared in Roar. This room is where magic happens.

While I pull the sari-covered camp bed into middle of the room, Win runs around picking up toys and flicking through comics. I take off the sari and rest my hands on the headboard. I stare at the letters that I scratched into the plastic years ago:

ENTUR HEER FOR THE LANED OF ROAR!!!

Even though Grandad's been looking after the camp bed for us, it still looks old and fragile. The mattress is sagging and the springs are covered in rust. Win runs past, bumping

into it, and I have a sudden urge to tie something big and strong round it. Rose has always said that if the bed is ever opened, everything inside will disappear . . . I push this frightening thought away. It's never going to happen. We're going to have Roar forever.

'Good horse!' says Win, and I look up to see him sitting on Rose's old rocking horse Prosecco. He rocks wildly, his knees up near his ears. If Win even tried riding the Prosecco in Roar he'd get thrown to the ground, stung repeatedly by Prosecco's boy-stinging tail and probably bitten. It's hard to believe that this rickety rocking horse brought the mighty

31

Prosecco in Roar to life . . . although they do have the same wild, staring eyes.

Grandad walks into the attic. 'All ready to go?' he asks, then he opens his arms wide. 'Come and give me a hug, twins. You too, Win.' We all bundle in and he squeezes us tight. 'I want you to promise to look after each other.'

'We will, Grandad,' I say.

'And keep an eye out for Crowky.' Grandad knows all about the traps Win has put in place, and the lookouts we've got spread across Roar. Just like Rose and Win, he thinks we've got Crowky covered; I'm probably the only person in this hug who's not one hundred per cent sure.

Rose wriggles out of Grandad's arms and pulls up the hood on her onesie. It's getting small and is covered in burn holes and rips that Rose has attempted to sew up. 'Can we go now?'

Grandad laughs and pats her furry head. 'I think this might be your last trip to Roar in this thing.'

'Bye, Grandad!' she says, then without looking back she pushes her head inside the folded mattress and wriggles forward until her body and legs are hidden too. Next comes the bit that still amazes me. When all of Rose is tucked inside the mattress the bed trembles, the springs creak . . . and Rose disappears.

Grandad starts clapping. 'Brilliant . . . It gets better every time!'

Win goes next, but only after he's given Grandad another

hug. 'Bye, Jay,' he says. 'Thanks for all the curries and telly and stuff.'

'You're very welcome, young man,' says Grandad.

'You'll come and visit me, won't you?'

'Of course!'

Win squirms into the mattress and vanishes almost straight away. Rose and I have to think about Roar to get there, but Win doesn't because it's his home.

Now it's my turn. I always feel bad when the moment comes to leave Grandad. He used to love our summer visits, but now Rose and I want to spend every moment we possibly can in Roar. 'Maybe next time we can hang out with you for a bit,' I say.

Grandad laughs. 'Don't you worry about me, Arthur. I'm perfectly content pottering around here, but your time in Roar is precious. You need to get going!'

Something about his words makes me hesitate. I imagine Grandad once we've gone, all alone in the house, pottering. Then I imagine Crowky pulling himself out of the bed, his button eyes darting around the attic.

Grandad must be able to tell what I'm thinking because he puts his hands on my shoulders and says, 'I'm going to be fine. Now hadn't you better catch up with Win and Rose?'

I give Grandad one last hug then kneel in front of the bed. I'm an expert at this now, but even so I feel a bit nervous. Less than an hour ago I pushed my head into Grandad's cupboard and found nothing but old wooden boards.

To get to Roar I have to believe, so I push these thoughts away, shut my eyes and wriggle forward. Before I've even pulled my feet in behind me I start picturing the dazzling colour of Roar's birds and the deep blue of the Bottomless Ocean. Then, when every bit of me is buried in the musty mattress, I lose myself in Roar.

I feel the heat of the dragons' fire as it rolls past my face, and I hear the crunch-crunch of my footsteps as I step in the snow at The End. I imagine I'm burying my nose in my unicorn Ronaldo's mane. It smells like summer: of dry grass and salt with a dash of coconut. It's an amazing smell. It's a Roar smell.

I inch my fingers forward. The mattress has gone and I can feel stone.

Now I start to crawl.

I know this tunnel well. I dip my head to miss a low hanging rock and move left to avoid the pool of water that always seems to be there. I move quickly, my eyes fixed on the green light up ahead where I can see Rose and Win waiting for me.

Win calls out, 'Hurry up, Arthur!' but his voice is drowned out by the sound of thundering water. The On-Off Waterfall is crashing past the mouth of the cave.

By the time I reach them the water has become a trickle and sunlight slips between the trailing leaves that cover the entrance of the tunnel.

'Ready?' says Rose.

We always go through the leaves together. Like putting our things in Grandad's fruit bowl, it's a Roar tradition.

'Ready,' I say, and together we push the leaves aside and crawl forward.

We come out on a narrow ledge in the middle of a cliff. From here we can see all the way across Roar, from the pool below us, past meadows and forests, and on to the Bottomless Ocean and the islands of the Archie Playgo. The sun is just beginning to go down and everything seems to glow. Even the nets that Win has hidden among the trees – traps to catch Crowky – gleam like spiders' webs spun from gold.

I point beyond the Bottomless Ocean to the line of snow-tipped mountains on the horizon. 'What do you think we'll find there?' I ask. Tomorrow we're going to sail through those mountains on our way to the mysterious islands.

'Who knows?' says Rose, laughing. 'It could be anything!'

Then she puts her fingers to her lips and whistles for her dragons.

CHAPTER 7

'Hobey, drobagobons!' calls Win. He's finally learned Rose's dragon language and is keen to try it out. 'Hobow obis obit gobobing?'

Vlad and Pickle ignore him and hover in front of the ledge. They're gazing at Rose through narrowed, glittering eyes and smoke is seeping out from between their teeth.

'Cobome clobosober, Pickle!' Rose demands.

Obediently ruby-red Pickle stretches his neck towards the rocky ledge. He huffs, happy to see Rose, and sparks shower over us.

We've decided to use the dragons to get down from the cliff because Win's done such a good job of booby-trapping the waterfall. As well as the nets hidden in the trees, he's also greased the stepping stones that jut out of the side of the cliff with something he calls 'unicorn wax'. Win claims he knows which steps are safe but Rose and I don't entirely trust him, which is why we're climbing straight on to the dragons' backs.

As Pickle inches closer and closer, I tell myself that it's going to be fine. After all, Rose has done this lots of times.

'Just copy me,' she says when Pickle's snout is almost touching the ledge. Then, without hesitating, she steps off the ledge and on to Pickle's large head. With her arms outstretched she walks along his neck and then sits down on his scaly back. 'See?' she says. 'Easy!' Then she whispers in Pickle's ear and with one great thrust of his wings – which nearly blows me and Win off the ledge – they turn and start to fly towards the Archie Playgo.

Now it's our turn.

Blue, craggy Vlad stares at us. His jaws gape open and with each breath he takes a blast of hot air rushes over our feet and legs.

Win steps back. 'Arthur, I'm thinking . . . maybe I'll use those greasy stepping stones?'

'No way,' I say, grabbing hold of him. 'If I'm doing this, then so are you.'

Vlad growls and smoke trickles from his nostrils. I force

myself to smile, then reach out a hand. 'Cobome hobere, plobease, Vlad.'

He flies a touch closer, but his snout is still quite a distance away. Just then I hear a rumbling sound. At first I think it's Vlad's stomach then I realise it's coming from above us. The On-Off Waterfall is about to turn on!

'Let's go,' I say, and I jump on to Vlad's lumpy head. Arms windmilling, I run along his neck then throw myself down on his back. I look up as a wave of water comes crashing over the top of the cliff. 'Hurry up, Win!'

Screaming, Win jumps on to Vlad's head and comes hurtling towards me. Water slams down and Vlad is so desperate to get away that he swings his neck round before Win has reached the safety of his back. I grab Win's cloak just as his feet slip out from under him and, as Vlad rises higher and higher, I'm the only thing stopping Win from plunging to the ground. Eventually he manages to scramble up behind me.

'Rose is right,' says Win, squeezing water out of his robe. 'That *was* easy!'

Vlad cuts through the sky, keen to catch up with Rose and Pickle. We're heading towards Mitch's island because that's where the *Alisha* is moored. We're going to sleep at Mitch's tonight and set sail first thing in the morning.

Win leans over Vlad's side and points to the ground. 'Look, Arthur. There's my cave.'

With a hand wrapped round one of Vlad's spikes I peer down and watch as we drift past Win's cave then over a patchwork of fields, rivers and mountains. We follow the twisting Rainbow River until it meets the sea and that's when I spot two unicorns grazing at the edge of a meadow. 'Win, is that Penguin and Ronaldo?'

'Oi, PENGUIN! RONALDO!' bellows Win, but of course the unicorns can't hear us all the way up here.

Looking down at the unicorns I see a strange sight. The meadow is dotted with holes. Some are huge, almost as big as craters. 'What are those holes?' I shout.

'The Lost Girls dug them,' says Win. 'Stella got fed up with the little ones mucking around in the Crow's Nest so she said she'd buried treasure in the meadow. They've been digging holes there ever since.'

'Has she really buried treasure down there?'

'Yes, a whole barrel of Marmite!' says Win excitedly. 'The honey badgers turned up on the *Bowt* and Mitch bought it for fifty loombands. I dug that massive one myself.'

The hole he's pointing at is so big it could easily be turned into a swimming pool. 'Nice work,' I say.

We leave the holey meadow behind us and catch up with Rose and Pickle over the Bottomless Ocean. Side by side the dragons fly into the setting sun. Rose is smiling and her brown skin glows as she leads the way on Pickle.

Soon the sea below us is peppered with tiny islands. 'We're nearly there,' Rose calls, pointing ahead to a round island. 'Get ready to land!'

Pickle dips his head and starts to glide lower. Vlad follows and I tighten my grip on his hot scaly sides. As the dragons circle the island, I spot the *Alisha* moored to one side. A mermaid skull and crossbones flag flutters from the tallest mast. Then I see small figures running around on the island. This is strange. With the exception of Rose, Mitch isn't keen on visitors. It's one of the reasons she lives in the middle of nowhere.

'Win,' I say, 'who's that on Mitch's island?'

'I think it's the Lost Girls,' says Win, as two of the figures start hitting each other with sunflowers. The others join in and we watch as one of them gets whacked into the lagoon. Yes, it's definitely the Lost Girls.

Suddenly Vlad lets out a growl and flames shoot across the sky. The Lost Girls look up and start jumping up and down and shouting. Win takes off his wizard's hat and waves it above his head, and that's when Vlad decides it's time to land. He dives sharply and Win's hat flies out of his hands.

'Hold on,' I shout as thick smoke blows in my eyes. 'It's going to be a bumpy landing!'

CHAPTER 8

Vlad skids to a halt at the very edge of the lagoon and Win and I are tossed over his head and into the water.

We splutter to the surface to the sound of loud laughter. It's Mitch. She's lying in her hammock, her tail and blue hair trailing in the lagoon. 'Well, if it isn't Arthur Trout, Master of Roar, and the mighty Wininja. What an excellent landing. Ten out of ten!'

'She is *so* sarcastic,' says Win, as we swim towards shore.

'Heard that,' says Mitch, and she rips some leaves off the tree, pulls a starfish out of her hair and chucks the whole lot in our direction. It must be a spell because in mid-air it transforms into green smoke and seconds later hundreds of tiny starfish fall down on us, prickling our skin.

'Now hurry up and get out of my lagoon,' she says. 'You're making it smell of boy and ninja wizard!'

We pull ourselves on to the deck as Rose appears round the side of the hut. It looks like her landing went very smoothly. She's surrounded by a gang of girls. Some of them are soaking wet, others are muddy. They're all wearing their usual collection of colourful T-shirts and leggings, and their arms are covered in loomband bracelets and something else . . . Tattoos. On their left shoulders they all have the same tattoo of a grinning skull with a ribbon perched on its head.

Rose runs forward and throws herself into Mitch's arms. For a moment she's hidden by Mitch's mass of blue hair, which today is encrusted with even more shells than usual and a lot of seaweed ribbons.

'Missed you!' cries Rose.

'Missed you too,' says Mitch. Then, just to show Rose how pleased she is to see her, she opens a vial that's hanging round her neck and pours the contents over Rose's head. Instantly Rose's hair becomes bright blue.

'You gave us matching hair!' says Rose.

'Because blue is the best,' says Mitch, then she shifts over so Rose can share her hammock.

'Mitch, have you been tattooing the Lost Girls?' I ask, shaking water from my ears.

'Yep. I do them in exchange for spell ingredients. You should see Stella's. It's a whopper.'

And that's when Stella, the leader of the Lost Girls, appears from Mitch's hut holding two mugs of something pink and bubbling.

'Oh, hello,' she says, as if Rose and me appearing in Roar is something that happens every day. Then she passes Mitch one of the mugs, adding, 'If you lot want a cup of pink, you'll have to make it yourself.' Her tattoo, I notice, covers the top of her left arm and most of her shoulder. It is indeed a whopper.

Win and I sit with Stella on the edge of the jetty and we all talk about the expedition. Mitch tells us what food she's planning to take and we discuss our route and how long it

will take us to reach the islands. This is when the Lost Girls decide we're being boring and go off to play with the dragons.

'Remember: don't stroke them backwards!' Stella shouts as they run across the meadow. 'And, Flora, *don't* blow in their ears. You know what happens.'

It soon becomes clear that Mitch is as excited as we are about returning to The End.

'I can't wait to be back on the open seas,' she says, gazing beyond the island to the best pirate ship I ever created:

the *Alisha*. We can see the orangutan crew lolloping about on board; several swing from the rigging and another looks like it's having a nap in the crow's nest. 'I've been out on a few practice sails,' Mitch adds, 'just to make sure I haven't lost my captaining skills – I haven't – and now I'm desperate for the cold and icebergs and *adventure*!'

Her words send a shiver of excitement running through me.

'Stella, don't you wish you were coming with us?' says Rose.

Stella shakes her head. 'No way. We're going back to the Tangled Forest to rebuild Treetops. Crowky's castle is cool but the sun never shines on the Bad Side. I don't know how Crowky put up with it.'

The Lost Girls used to live in a collection of tree houses hidden deep in the Tangled Forest until Crowky burned them down. Then they took revenge by invading his castle – the Crow's Nest.

Perhaps it's Stella's mention of Crowky, but something makes us all fall quiet.

'Stella, you'll keep an eye out for him, won't you?' I say, breaking the silence.

'It's all sorted, Arthur,' she says. 'We've got a lookout rota. There will always be two of us at the Crow's Nest ready to raise the alarm if he shows up. What will you do if you find him at The End?'

'Run!' says Win.

I shake my head. 'Not until I've got the T-shirt back.'

Rose laughs. 'You and that T-shirt, Arthur!'

'Sorry, but it's hard to relax knowing that Crowky's essentially got a key that will let him into Home.'

'No way,' chips in Win. 'That's not happening. Not with all the deadly booby traps I've set up. They're so good I've caught *myself* in them twice!'

Stella takes a long sip of her cup of pink, then says, 'I'll tell you one thing. If you *do* bump into Crowky out there, and he's got the T-shirt, he won't give it up without a fight.'

Her words hang in the air. From across the island we hear the Lost Girls screaming. A mermaid's head plops out of the lagoon then disappears again.

'He might if I use my powerful magic on him,' says Mitch.

'And if I add some of my equally powerful ninja moves,' says Win.

Rose shakes her head. 'We don't even need to think about it. We've got lookouts, booby traps and no one's seen him for months. We're about to have the best Crowky-free expedition ever!'

And just then, as the first rainbow stars appear in the sky, I realise she's right. This feels so different from our trips before. Everyone knows about the T-shirt and everyone is looking out for Crowky. Together we can keep each other safe.

Suddenly Mitch screams, 'I'm so flipping excited!' and she hugs Rose with such enthusiasm that they're both tipped out of the hammock and into the lagoon.

'WATER FIGHT!' shouts Win.

This isn't true, but his words bring Lost Girls running from all over the island and, before I know it, Audrey, the smallest Lost Girl, has yelled, 'Take that, Arthur!' and shoved me into the water.

And then there is a water fight. A massive one.

CHAPTER 9

That evening, after cups of pink and lots of toast, Win and I settle down by the fire in Mitch's hut. Something green is bubbling in her cauldron and I can hear the odd splash coming from the hole that's cut into the floor. Mitch uses this hole to get in and out of her lagoon, and it's why, right now, the room smells faintly of fish and pondweed.

The fire glows, and in the room next door I can hear Mitch and Rose whispering to each other and occasionally cackling with laughter. The Lost Girls are camping out in tents they've put up all over the island, and somewhere nearby Vlad and Pickle are snoring.

Here on Mitch's island, surrounded by my friends and with the dragons close by, I feel incredibly safe. A warm, calm feeling runs through me. *We are so lucky to have Roar,* I think, as my eyes close and drift off to sleep.

***

I'm woken at dawn by a cloud of hot smelly stars. 'Good morning!' says Mitch, dusting her hands over my head.

'OW!' I say, picking a star out of my ear and tossing it towards the hole in the floor. It hisses when it hits the water. Next to me, Win blows stars out of his nose.

'Whoops, did my potent magic just wake you up?' says Mitch, then she points at a pile of boxes and bags. 'Seeing as you're awake you might as well row this lot out to the *Alisha*.'

Win and I pick up some boxes and stumble out of the hut. The island is already buzzing with activity. The Lost Girls are packing up their tents and Rose is feeding doughnuts to all three of her dragons. Her hair, I notice, is no longer blue.

Bad Dragon must have turned up in the night because right now her colossal snout is stretched along the ground and she's gazing at Rose with a look of adoration. She's huge. Rose can only reach up to scratch her forehead by standing on tiptoes. Bad Dragon's jaw gapes and her needle-sharp teeth glint in the sun. If she felt like it, she could gobble Rose up, but my sister looks perfectly happy leaning against her and tossing doughnuts in her mouth.

Win and I make several trips across the island until the rowing boat is loaded with bottles of ingredients, blankets, food, binoculars and even a ukulele. Mitch's cauldron sits at the top of the pile, a wisp of ruby smoke floating out. We push the boat off the beach, then jump in.

The younger Lost Girls have gathered on the beach to wave goodbye. 'Bring us back a penguin!' shouts Nell.

'I hope you don't get eaten by a whale!' shouts Hannah.

'I hope you DO!' shouts Flora, and then they collapse with laughter.

As we row, merfolk raise their heads out of the water to stare at us. Like on Mitch, colourful tattoos cover their skin and they look like giant tropical fish as they circle our boat. I think they must be nudging us forward because soon we're drawing alongside the *Alisha*. Ropes are thrown to us and then the orangutan crew climb down and start grabbing the boxes.

'Hello,' Win says cheerily. 'Nice to see you again!' But the apes just curl their lips and grunt at him. We haven't got a clue what they're saying because, unlike Rose and Mitch, we don't speak Ape, but this doesn't stop Win from chattering away to them as we climb on board.

The orangutans clearly don't want our help, so while Win runs off to explore the ship I stand on deck and remember just how much I love life at sea. The sails are being released and they snap in the wind. At the stern Mitch's copper hot tub is ready for her and steam rises from the surface of the water. I kick off my shoes and feel the warm rough planks under my feet.

Win runs up to me. 'I've bagsied us two of the best hammocks!' he says, eyes shining, and then, because he's so excited, he pulls out his wand and shouts, 'Whistle fur!' making marshmallows explode across the deck.

We munch our way through the pile of marshmallows and watch as back on shore the dragons are persuaded to take the Lost Girls to the Tangled Forest. Rose goes with them, sitting on Bad Dragon with a row of girls packed behind her. She's planning to catch us up. Judging by the screams of delight coming from the Lost Girls, this is one of the best things that's ever happened to them.

'BYE, ARTHUR . . . BYE, WIN!' screams Hansini, leaning so far over Pickle's side that she almost slips off.

We set sail as soon as Mitch swims out to the *Alisha* and pulls herself on board. She has a quick dip in her hot tub, then sits on its copper edge and bellows to her crew, 'Unfurl the sails, me hearties! Let the expedition to beyond The End commence!' At least, that's what she claims she says; to us it sounds like a load of grunts.

Moments later the anchor is pulled up, the sails are all released and the huge ship begins to slip through the water.

Win and I run to the prow. In front of us lies a scattering of Archie Playgo islands then mile upon mile of open sea. In the distance, looking like a row of jagged teeth, are the mountains of The End. Until our last trip to Roar, The End was a mystery to us. We'd never visited and we didn't know what, if anything, lay beyond it, but now we know that Roar stretches far beyond those mountains.

A dark shadow swoops across the deck, followed by a clap like thunder. Smoke drifts over us. Rose has arrived on Bad Dragon. She flies ahead of the ship, leading the way, with Vlad and Pickle following just behind.

Win throws his arm round my shoulder and pulls out

his wand. 'Isn't this brilliant, Arthur? I feel like I should do another spell to celebrate the start of our expedition. Something big . . . Something *new* . . .'

'Like what?' I say nervously.

'Like this!' he cries, then he swings his wand through the air and shouts, 'WHIPPET CRISPS!'

CHAPTER 10

It takes a while to clear up all the spaghetti strung across the ship by Win's spell. It spiralled out of his wand like silly string, whipping Mitch in the face and knocking an orangutan off the rigging. The apes help us out by eating the strands tangled in their fur, and then Win and I pack the rest into a pan for dinner.

'It's just what I expected to happen,' Win says cheerfully as he tugs a piece out of my hair, 'because I absolutely love spagitty.'

'You've never eaten it before in your life, have you?'

'No,' he admits, 'but I know I'm going to love it. I mean, it's food *and* it's a weapon. Like apples!'

Soon we've sailed clear of the Archie Playgo and into the Bad Side of Roar. Rose still leads the way, sitting proudly on Bad Dragon's back. I guess she must be enjoying herself too much to join us down here on the boat.

As the dragons head towards the mountains we catch a glimpse of Crowky's castle, the Crow's Nest. It's hard to miss.

It sits on a jagged rock in the middle of the sea with waves smashing against its thick stone walls. Four twisted towers stand out against the grey sky like the stunted branches on a tree. I shiver and turn away. It's not just the sight of the castle that's made a chill run through me: the temperature has dropped. That's what happens when you get closer to The End.

The sea has become rougher too. Back in Home, waves like this would make me feel seasick, but this is Roar so I don't feel ill at all. In fact, I love the way the *Alisha* plunges down into each wave then rises back up to hover on the crest of the next one.

Eventually it becomes too cold for the dragons. Last time we visited we discovered that the icy air makes the fire in their bellies go out and then they crash towards the sea. Rose won't let that happen again, so we watch as she makes Bad Dragon turn round and then Vlad and Pickle follow her.

'How is she going to get into the boat?' asks Win. Right now Rose is a tiny figure perched on Bad Dragon's shoulders.

'I don't know,' I say, 'but I bet it's going to be dangerous.'

'Yep, she's going to jump,' says Mitch calmly, then she pulls herself out of the hot tub.

Above us Rose is clambering to her feet on Bad Dragon's back. She stands there for a moment, wobbling, then, as Bad Dragon swoops low over the ship she takes a running jump. 'HEAR ME ROAR!' she yells as she drops through the air. She lands in the middle of Mitch's hot tub, spraying us with

water. A moment later she emerges with a triumphant look on her face then says to me, 'Don't you dare tell Grandad!'

The dragons fly away with a series of screams and blasts of fire and we watch until they are just dots in the sky. Then they vanish. The second they are gone, I miss them. Nothing makes you feel safer than having a dragon by your side.

**

We reach the chain of mountains at sunset.

The cold has forced Rose, Win and me into our fur onesies and moon boots and we stand at the bow of the ship looking like polar bears. The orangutans gather round too. No one wants to miss the moment we sail through the mountains and into The End.

The snowy peaks tower ahead of us and silence falls over the ship. The narrow gap we're sailing towards is just wide enough for the *Alisha*. We've passed through it twice before, but never this late, when the light is fading and stars are already appearing in the sky.

'Look!' says Rose. A humped shape has risen out of the water alongside the ship. It's a furry whale, and really it belongs on the other side of the mountains at The End because that's where Rose and I sent the things we didn't want in Roar.

Whenever we played a game in Grandad's attic and something new appeared in Roar, we could either say 'For keeps!' – which meant it would stay in Roar for ever – or shout out 'Send it to The End!' We got rid of lots of stuff that gave us the creeps, but things we loved went to The End too. That's because we made Roar when we were little and annoying each other was a fun thing to do.

Rose loved her biting fairies so I sent them away; I loved furry killer whales so she returned the favour by yelling, 'Send them to The End!' the second she saw them. Rose banished loads of my creations. I think she enjoyed annoying me a bit too much.

'Look at it, Rose,' I say, as my whale arcs out of the water, its black-and-white fur trailing behind it. 'I bet you like my furry whales now!'

She shrugs. 'They're all right, I suppose.' Water sprays from the whale's blowhole. It's filled with phosphorescence and it lights up the sky like a glittering firework. 'OK, that's pretty good,' she's forced to admit.

Suddenly Mitch shouts, 'Hold steady!' and when we turn we see that the *Alisha* has reached the gap in the mountains. There's no turning back now!

Walls of rock rise around us. Win grabs my arm and an ominous groan comes from deep inside the *Alisha*. There is a scraping sound and then we're inside the channel, racing towards The End.

CHAPTER 11

The next morning, the first thing I see when I stumble on deck is a penguin. It squawks at me before flapping its stubby wings and flying up in the air. I rush to the side of the ship and watch as it gracefully dips into the sea to snatch up a fish. I laugh and bitterly cold air fills my lungs. Like most of the creatures at The End, flying penguins were one of my creations.

The *Alisha* glides slowly past huge icebergs and the sun glitters off their sheer sides. Behind me the ship is noisy with orangutans as they grunt instructions at each other, but the sea is eerily quiet. Pale fish swim below its glassy surface and trailing ribbons of weed drift by.

I shiver and pull my hood round my face. My eyes dart from the icebergs to the coast that we're sailing alongside. I'm looking for black wings or a hunched-over shape. I'm waiting to hear my name whispered on the icy breeze. No one has seen Crowky since we left him floating in the sea, but surely if he's anywhere, it's here?

'Arthur!'

I jump and look up to see Win peering down from the crow's nest. 'Grab some porridge and bring it up here!'

Hot porridge. *That's* what I need to take my mind off Crowky.

With a bowl tucked under one arm I climb to the top of the tallest mast and join Win in the crow's nest. I can't help feeling proud of myself as I settle down next to him. I used to be terrified of heights, but I just climbed a rope ladder like it was a set of stairs and I didn't spill a drop of porridge.

Win passes me the binoculars, saying, 'If you look over there, you'll see the islands.'

At first all I can spot is mile upon mile of blue sea. Then I pick out a speck of green. The swaying of the ship makes it disappear, but a second later it's back again. It's definitely an island and beyond it there are more!

I sit down next to Win to eat my porridge. 'It won't take us long to get there,' I say. 'We should be there before dark.'

'Ah, there's been a change of plan,' he says. 'We're going to make a detour to Barracuda Bay.'

'What?' I drop my spoon in my bowl. 'Win, why are we doing that? No one wants to go to Barracuda Bay. Not after what happened last time!'

Win shrugs. 'Don't blame me. It was the girls' idea.'

Barracuda Bay is an abandoned pirate village and the last time we visited we got tied up by a wolf-girl, then chased by Crowky and his scarecrow army. The village has one inhabitant: a surly bear called Carol Brocklebank who runs the very grubby Bucket of Blood inn.

I lean over the side of the crow's nest and see Rose and Mitch lounging in the hot tub. 'Ahoy down there!' I yell. 'Do we really have to go to Barracuda Bay?'

'Yes!' Rose shouts back. 'I want glögg. I've been thinking about it loads. I've got cravings, Arthur!'

Rose acts like her cravings are medical emergencies. Once she had a craving for a Flake so bad she couldn't sleep and she actually persuaded Dad to take her to an all-night garage to get one.

'Seriously? Glögg wasn't even that nice,' I say.

It was. It tasted like liquid honeycomb with a sprinkling of cinnamon and a smidgen of cream, but I'm not about to admit that.

'Pleeeeeease?' she says.

'Fine, but we're only popping in, right?'

She grins. 'Definitely!'

Win and I spend the rest of the morning up in the crow's nest, watching the coastline slip by. It's incredible. We see more flying penguins, whole pods of furry whales and other creatures too. Arctic foxes slink along the shoreline watching the *Alisha* with seaweed-green eyes and seagulls as colourful as parrots circle overhead. Of course I also keep an eye out for Crowky.

Win soon works out what I'm doing because I'm hogging the binoculars.

'He's not here, mate,' he says, clapping his hand down on my shoulder. 'He's gone.'

'I know,' I say, 'but I've got so used to looking for him, it's hard to stop.'

At around midday Mitch bellows up to us, 'Yo ho ho, me hearties, land ahoy!'

Win and I climb down from the crow's nest and join the others at the side of the ship.

'There it is,' says Mitch, her breath misting the air. 'Barracuda Bay!'

A ramshackle group of wooden buildings clings to the shoreline. Some are on solid ground but others are built on stilts over the sea. The tallest building by far is the Bucket of Blood. It stands over the rest of the village like a wonky tower, its sign swinging in the wind.

'What is *that*?' says Win. He's pointing at a strange collection of shapes by the shore. I lift the binoculars and realise that the shapes are actually figures covered in snow. Twig fingers stick out here and there and button eyes stare back at me. I'm already cold, but the sight of them sends

a chill running through my body because this is Crowky's
scarecrow army.

We take it in turn to look at them through the binoculars.

'Freaky,' Mitch mutters. 'They look like statues.'

'Really, really creepy statues,' says Win.

'Still need that glögg?' I ask Rose. I don't want to go
anywhere near those scarecrows. Crowky made them and
they can come to life. The last time I saw them they were
standing exactly where they are right now. They'd just chased
me and Win through Barracuda Bay but we managed to
escape by pedalo.

'Definitely,' Rose says, then she smiles. 'Don't you see,
Arthur? The fact that the scarecrow army are here, *exactly*

where Crowky left them, tells us that he's gone. He made those scarecrows and he'd never abandon them.'

'Rose is right, Arthur,' says Win. 'Those scarecrow dudes are Crowky's only friends.'

The four of us fall quiet as the *Alisha* moves closer and closer to land.

Rose nudges me. 'Barracuda Bay is safe, Arthur. Trust me. We'll have some glögg, chat to Carol and be on our way.'

CHAPTER 12

We use the small rowing boat to get to Barracuda Bay and Mitch swims alongside us. As I row, I keep my eyes glued to the scarecrows. They remain totally lifeless; the only thing that moves is their straw hair that blows in the wind. In fact, they're so still that when we climb out of the boat I'm confident enough to crunch through the deep snow with Win to check them out.

'See you in the Bucket of Blood!' calls Rose as she heads in the other direction.

The scarecrows are clustered together, their arms outstretched, their heads lolling. I walk between them watching for any sign of movement. But their stick fingers are still and their eyes look dull. I stop in front of one of the larger ones. It looms over me dressed in a ripped shirt and dungarees. Cautiously I reach forward and wipe the dusting of snow from its sack face. A stitched smile grins back at me. I pull its fabric eyelid down. The moment I take my finger off it pings open again.

This makes me jump, but after a moment I feel brave enough to give the scarecrow a shake. Snow tumbles from its shoulders and to the ground. It looks and feels like an ordinary straw-stuffed scarecrow, but I've seen these things move like they have blood running through their veins and a beating heart.

'Win,' I say, 'how do you think Crowky brought these things to life?'

'I haven't got a clue,' he says, then he takes a top hat off one of them and puts it on his head. 'What do you think?'

'It looks good,' I say. 'Distinguished.'

'*Nice* . . . What does "distinguished" mean?'

'Super-cool.'

'That's me all right,' he says, then he struts towards the Bucket of Blood, calling out, 'Mitch, Rose, check me out. I've got a new hat!'

The pub is extremely piratical: there are barrel seats, candles dripping wax over the tables and a smouldering fire. It smells of herring and the sea, which we can see through gaps in the floorboards. Behind the bar is a bear wearing a dirty flowery dress.

'Hello, Carol,' I say. She ignores me, spitting on to the cup she's holding and giving it a wipe with a rag. 'Have you seen Crowky around?' She frowns so I add, 'He's the boss of the scarecrows out there. He looks like them, only he's got wings.' Quickly she shakes her head. 'What about the scarecrows? Have they been like that since we left?' This time I get one short nod, then Carol bangs down the cup and raises one furry eyebrow. She's getting fed up with my questions. 'Two pints of glögg, please,' I say.

She grunts, showing her teeth, then takes another cup off a shelf. Once we've got our drinks, and paid with imaginary money – Carol's preferred currency – we join Rose by an open window. Mitch is lounging on a rock outside, her tail trailing in the sea.

'Pull up a pew, me hearties!' she says. 'Nice hat, Win.'

I sit down, take a sip of my drink and enjoy the lovely sensation of drinking a piping-hot sweet drink while freezing snow drifts over me. 'Happy now?' I ask Rose. She's already on her second glögg and her cheeks have a rosy glow.

'Yes!' she says. 'My craving is cured, and Carol says I can buy a couple of barrels for the expedition.' Along with speaking fluent Dragon, Mermish, Moonlight Stallion and Orangutan, Rose can also speak Bear.

We sip our drinks and take it in turns to look through Mitch's telescope at the islands. We can see them more clearly now. Compared to the white snowy scene surrounding us they look dazzlingly colourful. If I hold the telescope steady, I can even see golden sand and swaying palm trees. I adjust the focus on the telescope so that the nearest island comes into focus. I wonder what we will find on that little blob of green?

I'm pulled out of my thoughts by a strange sound. It's a deep hum, like an engine . . . but that doesn't make sense because there have never been any machines in Roar. Then I think: Crowky. He's an inventor. Could he have made a car or a motorbike, something that's speeding towards us?

My heart thumps as I put down the telescope. 'Can you hear that?' I say.

The others stop talking and listen too. Rose frowns. 'It's coming from outside the village.'

'And it's getting louder,' says Win.

We all stare at the path that leads between the ramshackle houses and out of the village. The humming stops then starts again. It's deep and throaty, and it reminds me of something . . . *but what?*

Mitch shivers. 'Is it just me or is that sound freaking you out?'

I know what she means. There's something about the hum that's making the hairs on my arms stand on end.

Suddenly Rose gasps. 'That's not a hum. It's a *purr!*'

And that's when a gigantic grey cat comes strolling into Barracuda Bay.

'Shiver me timbers,' whispers Mitch. 'It's Smokey . . .'

CHAPTER 13

We haven't seen Smokey for years. He originally leaped out of The Box, an ordinary-looking cardboard box that was packed full of fears. All the fears belonged to me and Rose and they would jump out one at a time, follow us around and generally terrify us. There was a clown, a tiny ghost vampire, bee-spiders . . . Then one day Smokey stuck his big furry paw out.

It was Rose who hated cats, especially fluffy ones like Smokey. He ran after her, purring and trying to rub against her. Rose wouldn't have liked a normal-sized cat doing this, but Smokey was, and still is, massive. Imagine a camper-van-sized fluffy cat with sharp teeth demanding strokes. That's what Rose had to put up with.

The only way we could get rid of our fears was by proving we weren't scared of them. Rose had to tickle Smokey's tummy for ages to get him to go away. We didn't have a clue where they went, but now we know Smokey ended up right here in Barracuda Bay.

He pads through the snow, his purr getting louder, his green eyes fixed on Rose.

'He is still into you,' I say.

She shudders. 'Yeah, thanks, Arthur, I had noticed.'

Smokey pauses to sniff at a top-floor window. Snow falls from the roof, making him sneeze. The sound sends an avalanche of snow thudding to the ground and he jumps back, startled.

'*Ahh*,' says Win. 'You've got to admit he's cute!'

Smokey turns back to us and meows. We can see right inside his pink mouth. His teeth are bright white and each one comes to a sharp point.

'OK, that was a bit less cute,' says Win.

Smokey meows again. Urgently.

We've never had a pet cat, but I've looked after our neighbour's and I know what that meow means: Smokey's hungry.

'Remember how he used to pounce on me?' says Rose.

'And bat you around,' adds Mitch. 'But you're not scared of him any more, right?'

Smokey steps closer.

'Not really,' says Rose, 'but I'm thinking maybe we should . . . get back to the ship?'

'Aren't we safer here?' I say, eyeing the rickety walls of the Bucket of Blood.

'Arthur, this place feels like it's made out of matchsticks,' she says, 'and Smokey's paws are gigantic.'

71

'Good point,' I say, then I bang down my cup of glögg and run towards the door. Win follows, but Rose stays where she is, gulping down her last mouthfuls of drink.

'*Rose!*' I say. 'We need to go!' I look out of the door. Smokey has started to trot towards the inn. His thudding paws make the boards beneath our feet tremble.

'Coming!' she says, but first she chucks two barrels of glögg out of the window where they land in the sea with a splash. 'Put these in the rowing boat, Mitch!'

'See you later, Carol!' Win yells as the three of us sprint out of the inn and start to slip and slide our way through the snow towards the rowing boat. Luckily it's close – we left it by the scarecrows – but the snow is deep and Smokey has dropped into a crouch. He reaches out one paw and a row of claws ping out.

'He's getting ready to pounce!' I yell as we push our way past the frozen scarecrows.

'MEEEEOOOOW!' snarls Smokey, then he leaps through the air.

I try to run faster but my feet shoot out from under me. Win hauls me up, but then we both fall down in the snow.

'Stop mucking around, you two!' shouts Rose. 'He's behind you!'

I stagger to my feet, but Win stays where he is.

'Get up!' I yell, tugging at his arm.

'I can't. He's got me!'

And that's when I see that Smokey's outstretched paw

is pinning Win's cloak to the ground. His chin rests in the snow and he stares at us with round unblinking eyes.

'Good boy, Smokey,' I say, as I try to pull Win's cloak free. 'You stay there!'

'Arthur!' hisses Win. 'Have you seen the size of his teeth?'

I have because Smokey has opened his mouth again in a sort of cat-grin. Those teeth look sharper than Bad Dragon's.

Suddenly the muscles on Smokey's back ripple and his fur stands on end. Any second now he's going to leap forward and land on us, but he's still got Win pinned to the ground. I have to do something!

I reach out a hand and grab the first thing I touch: a scarecrow's arm. I wrench it free and hurl it behind Smokey.

He can't resist. He spins round and goes chasing after it. This is our chance.

'Let's go!' I shout, pulling Win up. We run towards the boat.

Rose is already sitting there, waiting for us. 'Come on!' she yells. 'He's after you again!'

Win and I must be much more tempting than a lifeless straw arm. A meow rips through the air and snow showers down on us. I reach the shore and throw myself into the boat. Mitch wraps the rope round her hand and gets ready to swim. But where's Win?

I turn round to see that he's stopped running and is tugging something off a scarecrow . . . a waistcoat. Just as Smokey leaps forward it comes loose. Win gives a triumphant cry and waves it above his head as he runs towards us.

Smokey bounds closer, smashing through the last scarecrows. I cup my hands round my mouth and shout, 'JUMP, WIN!'

He jumps, but so does Smokey. Rose and I grab hold of Win just as Smokey's claws slice through the air.

'Go, Mitch!' yells Rose.

The boat shoots forward and Win crashes down next to us, cackling with triumph.

The big cat watches us from the shore as we zoom out to

sea. He tilts his massive head to one side and meows sadly. Then he throws himself down, squashing several scarecrows, rolls on to his back and starts wriggling in the snow.

'Maybe he just wanted a tickle . . .' says Rose.

Win's not listening. 'Guys, *look*!' He holds up the waistcoat. Smokey's claws have slashed three tears through the fabric. He laughs. 'How distinguished is *that*?' Then he throws himself back in the boat and sighs. 'That was the best fun I've had in ages!'

CHAPTER 14

Mitch gets the orangutans to weigh anchor straight away. The sails puff full of wind and then, with a lurch to one side, the ship turns and heads towards the islands.

We watch as Smokey prowls up and down the shore. He starts playing with the scarecrows, picking them up in his mouth and tossing them in the air. He hurls the one wearing dungarees into the sea then pounces on the fluttering sleeve of another. After a while Carol comes out of the pub with a huge bowl of something that's steaming. She puts it down in the snow and Smokey trots over to her.

'Is Carol giving Smokey *glögg*?' asks Rose.

'I think she is,' I say, watching as Carol gets a thank-you whole-body lick from Smokey that knocks her down in the snow. He meows in her face then goes back to his glögg.

Rose shudders. 'I'm glad we left when we did.'

'And I'm glad I've got this *imaginary* new outfit,' says Win, strutting up and down the deck. He's put his waistcoat on over his fur onesie and the top hat is perched on his head.

'You look ridiculous,' says Mitch.

'Says the person with a *tail*,' replies Win.

Mitch uses her tail to swoosh water from her hot tub in Win's direction. As it's flying through the air it turns into a huge snowball that smacks him in the face.

He whips his wand out. 'Raisin tool!' he shouts through a mouthful of snow and an average-sized snowball plops out of his wand – only it hits Rose between the eyes, not Mitch.

Mitch cackles with laughter as Rose turns to Win, her snow-caked eyes narrowed.

'I'm going up to the crow's nest!' says Win, and he runs to the nearest rope and starts to climb. 'Coming, Arthur?'

'In a minute,' I reply.

Mitch disappears down the hatch that leads to her cabin muttering something about 'doing an awesome cat tattoo.' Then Rose turns to me and says, 'You want to talk about The Box, don't you?'

I nod. Something has been bothering me since we saw Smokey and I'm sure Rose has been thinking about it too. 'We know that the things we sent to The End came here,' I say. 'They're all around us.'

On cue a weed-covered manatee bursts out of the sea and growls. I invented the weed-manatees, but Rose didn't like their teeth so she sent them to The End. The weed-manatee starts barking, showing chunky yellow teeth. She had a point.

'But Smokey came from The Box,' I say. 'When we overcame our fears and they went away we thought they

77

were gone for good, but what if they're all hiding out here, like Smokey?'

Rose gazes at the islands. 'I guess they could be,' she admits.

'We should try to remember everything that jumped out of The Box so we don't get any nasty surprises.'

And for the next half-hour that's exactly what we do: we have a Box-brainstorming session and write everything down on a piece of paper. Here's what we come up with:

The Dark – big black blob that followed Rose around

Hati Skoll and her wolves – scary girl hunter and her pack of wolves

Bee-spiders – yellow-striped, tiny, hundreds of them, buzzed

Ghost Vampire – small ghost vampire that tried to bite Rose (although it couldn't because it was a ghost)

Shoes – pair of black pointy shoes that tiptoed after Arthur

The Gloved Hand – similar to the Shoes, but it was a hand wearing a leather glove and it scurried

Bendy Joan – Rose's ancient gymnastics teacher who wore a bright blue leotard

Candyfloss – clown with yellow hair and massive feet. Tried to tread on Arthur

'There is one person on that list that I do not want to see again,' says Rose with a shudder. 'Bendy Joan.'

Bendy Joan was inspired by Rose's gymnastics teacher who was very old and yet spectacularly flexible. The Roar version was also ridiculously springy. She could jump to the top of a tree with one bound where she would wait, perched like an owl, for Rose to go past. Then she would jump on top of her. She never did anything mean. She was just very surprising.

'I bet you're scared of seeing Candyfloss,' says Rose, and she can't help laughing because even though I found Candyfloss terrifying, Rose and everyone else in Roar thought he was hilarious.

'Actually, I've got over my clown thing,' I say. 'It's the Shoes that really give me the creeps.'

'Pitter-patter . . . pitter-patter,' says Rose, making her moon boots drum on the wooden boards.

'No, it was more: tip-tap . . . tip-tap . . . tippetty-tap-tap.'

Rose grins. 'You're right!' She studies the piece of paper before tucking it in the pocket of her onesie. 'Don't worry, Arthur, if those shoes come tip-tapping after you, I've got your back.'

'Same with Bendy Joan,' I say, then I slam my hands down on her shoulders and screech, 'STRETCH, ROSE, STREEEEETCH!'

The rest of the day is spent in the crow's nest with Win. It's become our place to hang out. Rose and Mitch have a spacious captain's cabin and hot tub; we have a cramped crow's nest. Still, the views are incredible, and it means that while Win tries out new spells, I can keep an eye out for Crowky.

I gaze through the binoculars, tracking the waves and floating chunks of ice, but all I see are penguins, more manatees and a lot of furry whales. As the hours drift by and we sail closer to the islands it seems impossible that Crowky could have got this far by floating in the sea. I find myself looking through the binoculars less and less and spending more time trying to keep cool.

The weather changes gradually. First the flurries of snow stop, and then the icebergs disappear. Next the thick clouds fade away to reveal blue sky. In the late afternoon we discover the crow's nest is a real suntrap and we have to drop our moon boots and then our fur onesies over the side. Down on the deck the orangutans find shady spots to snooze in and Mitch pours a potion into her hot tub that turns it into a cold tub.

We reach our first island late in the afternoon. We gather at the front of the ship to stare at what appears to be a perfect treasure island. It has sandy beaches and swaying palm trees. Birds hover above the trees and a waterfall tumbles over a cliff and splashes into the sea.

'We're here,' says Rose, 'further than we've ever been before!'

In my pocket I feel the soft edges of the map. Rose and I made it years ago and I brought it with us in case it helped us when we were sailing through The End. It's no use to us now. We've in an unmapped part of Roar and have travelled beyond everything we know. Once this thought would have scared me, but right now, standing here with my friends, I'm filled with excitement wondering what secrets these islands hold . . .

'Is anyone thinking what I'm thinking?' says Rose.

'That you really need a wee?' says Win, eyeing the gushing waterfall.

'*No*,' says Rose, 'that this is the perfect opportunity for a barbecue on the beach.'

Mitch throws her arm round Rose. 'You have the best ideas, ship-mate! Let's load up the rowing boat.'

CHAPTER 15

M itch claims she's too hungry to wait for us to row, so she grabs the rope and drags our boat to shore. I'm squashed between two orangutans. After our experience with Smokey we've decided to bring them along for protection. They smell of salt and straw and their long ginger hair tickles my arms; I fight the temptation to stroke them. If I did, I'm pretty sure they'd break my arm or throw me overboard.

We fall quiet as we approach the island, scanning the beach for any signs of life . . . or clowns or buzzing stripy spiders. When the boat hits a sandbank Mitch's head pops out of the water.

'Time for you lot to get out and walk,' she says.

I don't need to roll up my jeans: I cut the bottoms off a few hours ago when it got so hot in the crow's nest that Win started magicking up snowballs. I jump out of the boat into cool water, then together we haul the boat ashore.

The island is beautiful. Perfect. I step on to hot sand and gaze up at the tall palm trees that fringe the beach. They sway, creaking and rustling, and the air is filled with the smell of coconut, but this is Roar so, of course, this isn't an ordinary island. The sand has a sparkly golden shimmer and brightly-coloured shells are scattered across it. I pick one up. It's bright pink with a black spot in the middle. It looks like a Liquorice Allsort.

'I'll secure the boat,' says Mitch. 'You lot go and look for anything that might ruin our barbecue. Or eat us.'

In silence we walk up the beach and into the shade of the trees. Here we discover that the coconut smell is coming from yellow flowers that dangle from the branches. Rose picks one and puts it in her hair. Win copies her. So do the orangutans.

I hold one of the flowers in my hands: it's thick and waxy and, up close, the coconut smell is overpowering. I can remember the games that led to Win, Crowky and almost everything else in Roar appearing, but all this feels brand new.

'Rose,' I whisper, 'can you remember making this place up in a game?'

'Not really,' she says, staring at a bright green beetle that's crawling over her arm, 'but we did like pretending the sofa was an island. Perhaps all this came from a game we forgot about?'

I look around me. Thick creepers climb the trees and strange chatters echo down from the canopy. Is that what this place is? A forgotten game? And if that's true, what else

might we find here?

One of the orangutans pushes past me, climbs a tree
and starts swinging from branch to branch. The other one
follows and they disappear into the jungle.

'Arthur, look at this!' Win steps out from behind a tree
with a small red monkey wrapped round his neck. It's

covered in black spots. 'I've got a monkey and it looks like a *ladybird*!'

The monkey stays glued to Win until the barking of the orangutans sends it shooting up into a tree. The orangutans crash back through the leaves, flashes of orange fur lighting up the gloom of the forest. Ignoring us they head straight to the beach where they chatter excitedly to Mitch.

'What's happened?' calls Rose. 'Have they found something?'

Mitch grins. 'Nothing at all except for a lot of cute spotty monkeys. I declare this island safe!'

After a bit more exploring we make a fire close to the water's edge and start our barbecue. While the sun sets we eat corn on the cob, pink prawns and bananas stuffed with chocolate. Well, Mitch doesn't eat the prawns. She has a policy of never eating anything with a tail.

Afterwards we sit by the fire and watch the sun sink lower in the sky. The dark sea stretches away in front of us. It's a calm night and only the smallest waves roll up the beach and over Mitch's tail; rainbow stars glitter on the sea like jewels, or, in Win's opinion, 'really tempting pick-and-mix'.

'We should get back to the *Alisha*,' says Rose with a yawn. Arranged next to her are some treasures she's found on the island: a few shells, the skeleton of a fish and a stone that glows in the dark.

I wriggle my toes into the still warm sand. 'I wish we could sleep out here.'

'Me too,' says Mitch, 'but we'd better not. It's safer on the *Alisha*.'

I know Mitch is right, but it's hard to believe anything bad could live on this beautiful island.

'There's something we need to do before we go,' says Win, and then he swishes his wand through the air and shouts, 'Whistle fur!'

Marshmallows rain down on us. They fall in the orangutans' fur and land in the fire, filling the air with the smell of burnt sugar.

Mitch puts one on a stick and starts to turn it over a flame. 'That, Win,' she says, 'is an exceptionally good spell.'

Her words make him so happy that he stuffs three marshmallows in his mouth then leaps up and cartwheels into the sea.

CHAPTER 16

For the next few days we cruise round the Bends.

This is the name Win gives the islands because they're 'beyond The End'. Mitch and Rose say it's a stupid name, and I agree, secretly, but because we can't come up with anything better, it sticks.

Our days fall into a routine. Porridge – in the crow's nest for me and Win – followed by trips to two or three different islands. Sometimes the islands are so close to each other that we can row between them, or even swim, but usually we use the *Alisha* as our island taxi service.

When we arrive on an island a couple of orangutans check that it's safe, then we split up and explore. Win and I take the middle of the island while Rose and Mitch circle the coastline and investigate any rivers. Sometimes we meet up in a pool at the bottom of a waterfall or halfway down a river, and if this happens, we have what Mitch calls 'a good old fashioned skirmish', which is basically a fight.

What we fight *with* depends on what each island has to

offer. We have water fights, mud fights, squashy-exploding-apple fights and golden-slime fights. It's me who finds the golden slime hidden inside massive seed pods. We have a brilliant time chucking handfuls of the stuff at each other until we discover it's impossible to wash off and that it leaves us with glittery skin and hair. Win claims that this makes him look extra distinguished and fills a jar with slime so he can keep glittering when we're back in Roar.

Even when Mitch is mashing mud into my face, I don't think I've ever been happier. Our days are full of sunshine and skirmishes, and the islands are bursting with treasures waiting to be discovered. One has a pool hidden among the trees that's filled with spinning water. We jump in to cool off and drift round and round until we feel sick. This island also has coconuts with bright pink flesh that tastes of seaside rock and on the neighbouring island we find hot springs and huge sand dunes that we can roll down into the sea.

After each long day spent island-hopping we sit on the sun-warmed deck of the *Alisha* and show each other the souvenirs we've found: leaves that smell of chocolate cake, perfectly round pebbles made of coloured glass or a shell that contains a blob of gold instead of a pearl. Mitch builds up a collection of new ingredients for her spells and Win has a box dedicated to all the unusual fruit that he's discovered. Apparently Grandad introduced him to smoothies and now he's keen to create the ultimate Bends smoothie.

Rose's greatest discovery is a red stone that she finds on

the first island. Silver crackles have appeared on it and she's convinced it's a dragon's egg that has been waiting for her touch to 'come alive'. She insists on keeping it with her at all times, cradled in a net bag slung over her shoulder, and she whispers encouraging words to it, like, 'Mummy's here . . .' and 'Who's a big brave dragon? You are!' Whenever I catch her doing this I remind her that she's almost certainly talking to a stone, then she gives me an annoying smile and says, 'Just you wait and see, Arthur!'

Occasionally, when I'm floating down a silent river, or my feet are sinking into the sand on an untouched beach, uneasiness creeps through me because I haven't thought about Crowky or the fears that came out of The Box for hours. I try to stay on guard, but we've visited loads of islands now and not seen a single buzzing spider or black feather.

We all start to relax and on the third day of island-hopping we leave our orangutan bodyguards behind and even decide to camp out on the last island we visit.

We find a mossy rock pool perfect for keeping Mitch's tail wet and build a bonfire next to it. Then Mitch plays her ukulele and we talk long into the night.

Eventually Win falls asleep and Mitch goes off for a moonlit swim. Rose lies back on the sand and says what I've been thinking. 'I don't think any of our fears made it to the Bends, Arthur.' She lifts up her hand and turns it in the light of the stars. 'I don't think Crowky did either.'

'But he must be somewhere,' I say, and my words make

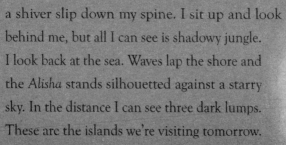

a shiver slip down my spine. I sit up and look behind me, but all I can see is shadowy jungle. I look back at the sea. Waves lap the shore and the *Alisha* stands silhouetted against a starry sky. In the distance I can see three dark lumps. These are the islands we're visiting tomorrow.

'Crowky could be on any one of those islands,' I say, 'and so could our fears . . .'

Rose laughs. 'You're such a funge, Arthur. I pointed out some good news, but like the fun sponge you are, you found something to worry about. You should be called Arthur McFunge . . . who lives in Funge Street . . . in the town of Fungely-on-Funge.'

'Yeah? Well, you should be called Rose Mc—'

'Mc *what?*' she says, throwing a clump of seaweed at me.

But I just smile and shrug because I've realised she's right: I'm in paradise and our fears and Crowky are nowhere to be seen. What am I worrying about? The unpleasant feeling disappears as quickly as it came . . . but obviously I still need to insult my sister. 'You should be called Rose McPoo-Head,' I say, 'from Plop-Plop-on-Sea.' And I throw the seaweed right back at her.

CHAPTER 17

We wake up on our fourth day of cruising the Bends to an unusual sight: clouds.

We gather by Mitch's hot tub while she takes long, deep sniffs of the air. 'Weather's on the turn,' she says.

It might be cloudy, but it's still hot, and nothing is going to stop us from visiting another island, especially as the one we're sailing towards looks so tempting. It's the largest so far, and it looks like a green dolphin rising out of the sea.

I mention this to the others, but Rose shakes her head and says, 'No. It looks more like a shark.'

'Whatever it is, Arthur and I are definitely climbing the fin,' says Win, pointing to the middle of the island.

Win's 'fin' is actually a mountain that's covered in trees except for a bald patch at the very top. We'll be able to see for miles from up there.

We get to Dolphin-Shark Island by rowing boat. To begin with, Mitch swims alongside us while I row, but after a while she gets impatient, grabs the rope and starts to pull us to shore. Like us, she wants to get there as soon as possible because we've decided we have to go back to Roar tomorrow. After we've been to this island we have two more to visit and then we're turning round. None of us wants to leave, and we're sure there are more islands out here, but we don't know how long it will take us to sail back and we want to spend a few days hanging out with the Lost Girls and doing all the other things we love, like visiting Boulders and Waterfalls and riding unicorns.

When we reach the island, we secure the boat, then Win and I head towards the jungle.

'Don't be long,' says Rose, shading her eyes from the bright sun. 'Remember we've got two other islands to visit.' The sun has made Rose's skin even darker than usual, and round her wrists and ankles she's wearing jewellery made from the shells she's found. Slung across her chest is the net bag that contains her so-called dragon's egg. She claims that she has to keep it close to her heart if it's going to hatch. When I rolled my eyes at this she said, 'It recognises the heartbeat of its mother, Arthur!'

'See you later,' I say. 'Look after that stone!'

'It's a dragon's egg!' she shouts as she runs into the sea to join Mitch.

Win and I walk into the cool, dark jungle. 'Ready to climb the fin?' asks Win with an excited smile.

The air is thick with heat and the chatter of birds and insects. We're about to set off when I see a dark shape moving between two trees. 'What's that?' I say.

Instantly Win drops into a crouch and stares hard. He stays like this for a moment then says, 'It's a leaf, Arthur. A really big green leaf.'

'Oh yeah!' I say, and we start walking, keeping our eyes peeled for any more deadly leaves.

I lead the way, pushing through vines and flowers until we find a smooth path that leads up the mountain. As usual, Win runs around gathering fruit. When we're halfway up I find something crumbly and brown scattered across the path. I rub it between my fingers. It feels a bit like wet sand and smells faintly of cinnamon.

'What do you think this is?' I ask Win.

'Some weird bird poo?' suggests Win.

I throw it to the ground and we keep climbing until we come out of the jungle and can scramble up rocks and on to the bald patch at the top of the island. The view from up here is incredible. Deep blue sea stretches into the distance and below us we can see Rose and Mitch lying on a rock. It doesn't look like they got any further than the next beach. We jump up and down and shout, but they can't hear us all the way up here.

Win takes out his binoculars and starts to turn round, checking out the whole of the island. When he's got his back to me he says, 'That's strange.'

'What's strange?'

'Well, Rose and Mitch are on a beach near the rowing

boat, so how come I can see footprints on the other side of the island?'

'Let me see,' I say, and he hands me the binoculars.

After a moment I find the marks he's talking about. They make a wobbling line across an otherwise empty beach. I fiddle with the focus until they stand out crystal clear. My heart thuds and I feel a prickle of fear. 'Win, there are *two* sets of footprints!'

'I know,' he says. 'I guess Rose and Mitch must have gone round there really quickly.'

'Win, there are *two* sets of footprints and Mitch doesn't have feet!'

All of a sudden this beautiful island seems a lot less friendly. Birds screech in the jungle below us

and waves smash on to the rock my sister and Mitch are lying on. I stare at the footprints. We've seen monkeys, parrots and lots of beautiful insects on the other islands, but never anything with feet. Something about this feels wrong.

'What should we do?' whispers Win.

I stick the binoculars in my pocket and start to scramble down the rocks, back the way we've just come. 'We find Mitch and Rose and we get off this island!' I say.

On our way down the mountain I see things that I missed on the way up. I spot a pile of logs hidden under a tree and a dropped apple core that has had slices cut out of it. And then, of course, there's the smooth path we're running along. None of the other islands had paths; we had to push our way through thick jungle and climb over trees. When I mention all this to Win, he says, 'Could be rabbits?'

'What? Collecting wood and cutting apples with a knife?'

'Maybe they're clever rabbits?'

We're out of breath and sweat is dripping down our faces, but we don't slow down. We run faster and faster, skidding on pebbles and using vines to swing round corners. We reach a straight bit of path and speed up. Then it happens. One moment my feet are touching the ground, the next something cuts into my ankles and I'm flying through the air. A scream tells me that Win has tripped up too. We land in a heap on top of each other.

'Invisible tripwire,' says Win, impressed. '*Stealthy!*'

'Win . . . Your wand is sticking in my ear.'

'Sorry, mate,' he says, jumping up and helping me to my feet. Suddenly he freezes and looks into the trees.

'What is it?' I say.

'I think I heard something.'

Side by side, we gaze into the dark forest. Win brandishes his wand and shouts, 'Come out . . . We're not scared of you!'

I am. Right now I am massively scared of whatever is hiding from us. Because as I stare into the shadows I realise that there's definitely something, no, *lots of things* hidden in the trees. I see the gleam of eyes and pale brown faces disguised by hoods. A twig snaps and when I spin round I see more eyes staring at me.

My heart thuds faster as I try to think of any hooded creatures that Rose or I sent to The End, but my mind has gone blank because, slowly but surely, the figures are stepping out of the jungle.

CHAPTER 18

'What *are* they?' says Win, pressing closer to me. The robed figures creeping towards us might be small, but there are lots of them. Some hold sticks, others have wooden swords clutched in their hands. I say hands, but they're unlike any hands I've ever seen before. They're smooth and fingerless and –

'AAAARRGGHHH!'

The scream comes from above us and I look up to see one of the creatures flying through the air on a vine. Its hood falls back, and that's when I realise who is attacking us.

'NINJABREAD MEN!' I shout.

The biscuity ninja lets go of the vine and shoots towards us, hands outstretched.

Win and I don't stop to think. We turn and we run, but after a few steps our path is blocked by another pack of robed ninjabread men.

'This way!' shouts Win, veering to the right. I follow him

down a narrow path, but soon this path runs out and we find ourselves standing on the edge of a small ravine. We're trapped. There is a drop in front of us and the ninjabread men are behind us.

Win's not giving up. He grabs hold of a dangling vine and launches himself over the ravine. 'Follow me,' he calls. 'We can swing to the other side!'

The vine holds his weight for a couple of seconds and then it snaps and he crashes into the jungle, disappearing from sight. I hear branches snapping followed by a loud 'OWWW!'

I glance over my shoulder. The ninjabread men are creeping towards me, their currant eyes narrowed, their swords outstretched. There are loads of them, too many to count, so despite what's just happened to Win, I grab my own vine and I jump. The vine doesn't break and I hurtle straight towards the other side. I don't believe it . . . This might just work!

But just when I'm about to jump to safety, the vine snags on a branch and I start to swing back . . . straight towards the waiting ninjabread men.

'You're going the wrong way, Arthur!' Win's voice echoes out of the jungle somewhere below me.

'I know!' I yell, but there's nothing I can do to stop myself from racing towards them.

I watch as they cackle with glee and start to jump up and down.

'LET GO!' shouts Win.

And even though this seems like a really, really bad idea, I do.

I crash through leaves and branches and land with a painful thud. My breath is knocked out of me, but before I can check if I've actually hurt myself, Win appears. 'This way,' he says, dragging me forward. 'I've found a path. If we're quick, we can get away!'

But the ninjabread men are already coming after us. We can hear twigs snapping and their excited cries.

'Come on!' shouts Win, and we run along a twisting path.

The sounds of the ninjabread men fade away. 'I think we've lost them!' I say, but no sooner are the words out of my mouth when a group of ninjabread men burst out of the trees ahead of us, blocking our way.

Win's right. They are stealthy.

They scream and snarl and thrust their wooden swords towards us. Seconds later the rest of the pack appear behind us. This time we really are surrounded.

'You can leave this to me, Arthur,' says Win.

'Are you sure?' I say. 'Because your last idea didn't go so well.'

'Yes,' he says, his voice brimming with confidence. 'I've been training for this moment all my life.'

I don't think I've ever seen Win move so fast. He leaps through the air in a flying tiger kick and his foot slams into the chest of the nearest ninjabread man, who collapses in an explosion of crumbs. I only see this for a moment because suddenly one drops down from above, landing on my back and wrapping its biscuity fingers round my face. I get a brief, delicious taste of ginger and syrup before Win knocks him off me. For the next few minutes Win whirls around the clearing, throwing punches and kicks in all directions. His hands are a blur and soon crumbs and wooden swords are scattered across the jungle floor.

One of the tiny biscuity ninjas leaps at my face and I get the briefest glimpse of currant eyes and an icing snarl before Win smacks him off, yelling, 'Leopard paw punch!' He swings round using his hand to knock down three in one go.

Win is on fire, and it isn't long before we're surrounded by broken biscuit. The ninjabread men must realise they are beaten because on some unspoken signal they retreat, slipping into the jungle as quietly as they came.

Win turns to face me, eyes wide. In his hand he's holding a gingerbread foot.

'Arthur,' he whispers, 'I've often wondered what would happen if I ever met an enemy as well trained and ruthless as me . . . and now I know. Total. Carnage.' Then he licks his lips – the ninjabread men do smell very tasty – and stares at the foot. 'What shall I do with this? Eat it?'

'No, leave it,' I say. 'He might come back and get it. Maybe he can stick it back on.'

'Stick it back on? What with?'

'I don't know . . . icing? It doesn't matter; you can't steal

body parts, Win,
even if they are
made of biscuit. Plus they
must have some way of gluing
their broken pieces back together.
There'd be nothing left of them
otherwise. Look how brittle they
are.' Suddenly I realise that the
sandy stuff I found earlier wasn't
weird bird poo, but left-behind
ninjabread men crumbs.

'They weren't brittle, Arthur,' says
Win. 'They were tough . . . like steel
or Mitch's tail.'

The clearing is littered with crumbs and biscuit fragments, evidence of the ninjabread men's extreme fragility, but I don't want to ruin Win's moment of glory, so I say, 'You're right. The one on my back weighed a ton. But you still shouldn't eat the foot. Eating your enemy is the sort of thing a monster would do, and you're not a monster, Win. You're a ninja wizard who follows a strict code of conduct.'

'Yeah, I suppose you're right,' he says, staring at the foot. 'But it smells so good!'

'Come on,' I say. 'Let's get out of here.'

We start to jog down the hill, keeping an eye out for ninjabread men as we go. I'm limping after my fall and Win is wincing with each step he takes, but we don't hang around. Both of us have had enough of this jungle.

'Hey, Arthur,' says Win after a few minutes. 'At least we know who made those footprints!'

The footprints . . . In all the excitement I'd forgotten why we were running through the jungle in the first place. I think about the footprints we saw on the beach and then I picture the ninjabread men's blob-shaped feet. Could they really have made those marks on the sand? I'm not so sure.

Ignoring the jabbing pain in my ankle I pick up speed. We have to find Rose and Mitch.

CHAPTER 19

We plunge out of the trees and on to the beach. Bright sunlight blinds me for a second, then I spot Rose and Mitch at the water's edge.

'We've got to get out of here!' I shout. 'We're not alone on this island. We just got attacked by ninjabread men –'

'Who I *destroyed*,' interrupts Win.

'It's true, he did, but someone else is on this island. We've seen footprints in the sand!'

I'm expecting Rose to be startled by this news, but she just laughs and says, 'And I know who made them!'

And that's when I realise that Rose and Mitch aren't alone. Sitting in the water next to them, and letting the foamy waves wash over her, is a small girl.

I shade my eyes from the sun and the figure jumps to her feet and grins, revealing a row of sharp teeth. 'Rose, is that one of your *fairies*?' I say.

Rose smiles happily. 'You may have sent them to The End, Arthur, but we found this one right here on this island!'

Rose invented four fairies when we were playing in Grandad's attic, but they weren't sweet innocent things who flew around caring for sick unicorns and collecting dew. No, Rose's fairies fought epic battles and were capable of powerful magic. They didn't even have wings because Rose always insisted that 'real fairies don't fly'.

I found Rose's fairy game annoying, and quite scary, so I wasn't happy at all when the fairies turned up in Roar. Rose begged me to let them stay, and I did for a few days, but then one of them bit me and I shouted, 'Send them to The End!' and the next time we visited, they were gone. Rose was furious that I'd banished her beloved fairies and we had one of our biggest-ever rows about it. Looking at this little fairy now, as she sucks on a piece of seaweed and gazes up at me through long eyelashes, I don't know why I was so frightened of them.

'Her name is Pebble,' says Mitch, then she wraps her tattooed arms round Pebble and gives her a squeeze. 'Isn't she adorable?'

I'm not sure I'd call Pebble adorable. She has bizarrely big eyes that give her the look of a bush baby, smooth skin the colour of a brown egg, wispy hair . . . and very sharp teeth. Can you ever call someone with sharp teeth adorable?

Pebble stares at me with those big unblinking eyes until I feel so uncomfortable that I have to say something. 'Um . . . hello!'

She doesn't reply. She just keeps staring, and that's when

I notice that colourful fish are circling round her ankles in the water. 'Pebble hasn't said a word to us,' says Rose.

'They used to talk all the time,' I say, remembering how the fairies would chatter away to Rose, talking over each other.

'She's drawn pictures, though,' says Rose. 'Look!' She points and I see that Pebble has drawn a boat and two islands in the sand.

'What does it mean?' I say.

Before Mitch can reply, Pebble runs out of the sea, grabs a stick and shoves me out of the way. Unlike the ninjabread men, she really does have iron strength, and her push makes me fall backwards.

Rose laughs. 'Fairies are strong, Arthur, remember?'

Next Pebble starts jabbing at the pictures with her stick, drawing a line from one island to the boat, and then on to the next island.

'We think she's saying she came here on a boat,' says Rose.

Pebble nods enthusiastically.

'But where are the other fairies?' I say. 'There were four, weren't there?'

'That's right!' says Rose. She's clearly delighted to be talking about her fairies again. 'They were all brothers and sisters. The others were called Twig, Moss and Owl. They were super-fast and strong and each one had a special power.'

I glance back at Pebble. She's sitting on the ground letting crabs run over her hands. 'So what's your special power, Pebble?'

Pebble looks at me and slowly mimes zipping her mouth shut.

'You mean it's a secret?' I say.

She smiles and nods.

'Arthur, fairies *never* share their secret powers,' says Rose, rolling her eyes. 'You'd know that if you'd ever bothered to read my Fairy Fact File.'

Ah, yes, Rose's Fairy Fact File. I'm starting to remember why I found the game so annoying. The fact file was a booklet Rose made where she wrote down all sorts of rules as if she was some sort of professor of fairies. She was even bossier than usual when we played fairies, stopping the game to say stuff like, 'Fairies *never* do that, Arthur! Don't you know anything?'

Pebble is still staring at me with her mouth clamped shut.

'But, Rose,' I say, 'you wrote the fact file, can't you remember her secret power?'

She laughs. 'No, I've forgotten . . . Perhaps it's crab-whispering? Look, she's covered in them!'

It's true. Now there are even more crabs crawling up Pebble's arm and some have made it into her hair.

Win laughs. 'Worst magical power *ever!*'

'What about the others?' I say, remembering that there were two sets of footprints on the sand. 'Have you seen them?'

'Not yet,' says Rose.

At the mention of her brothers and sisters Pebble stops humming and her large eyes become even larger.

Mitch wriggles out of the sea towards her. 'Did something happen to them, Pebble?'

Pebble shuts her eyes and shakes her head, as if she doesn't want to even think about it, then she grabs my hand and Rose's and starts dragging us towards the trees. Win follows. So do a couple of crabs.

'Oi!' shouts Mitch. 'Where are you going?'

'I don't know!' I reply, trying and failing to pull my hand out of Pebble's tight grip, but it's impossible. This little fairy is not letting go.

CHAPTER 20

Pebble leads us to a clearing in the forest where there's a wooden hut with a wisp of smoke drifting from a chimney and a starfish stuck to the door. There's also a garden and a swing tied to a tree. Pebble lets go of our hands and stands proudly by the hut. She points at her chest then gestures to the hut.

'Did you make it?' I say, and she nods enthusiastically.

'Nice,' says Win. 'Look, she's used her boat to make the roof.'

An upturned rowing boat sits on top of the hut. There are still a few barnacles clinging to the hull.

Pebble opens the hut door and disappears inside. Then she sticks her head out and beckons us. Win goes inside straight away and Rose goes to follow, but I hang back.

'What's the matter?' says Rose. 'You're not still scared of her, are you? Arthur, she's obviously harmless. Look, she's growing carrots!'

Not only is Pebble growing carrots, but she's also painted

a carrot label on a shell to mark her crop. Can a fairy who makes carrot labels be a threat? Possibly, I decide, as I step into the hut.

In the dim light I see a bed on the floor covered in leaves, some wood stacked next to a stove and a shelf covered with bits and bobs. While Win and I look around, Rose starts talking to Pebble, asking her yes and no questions. Following Pebble's nods and shakes of her head, we discover that Pebble eats fish that she catches and fruit from the forest.

'Find out who left the second set of footprints,' I say.

But when Rose asks if anyone else is on the island Pebble stubbornly shakes her head.

Rose turns to me. 'See? No one else is here, Arthur. You must have made a mistake.'

I pull Rose to one side. 'I saw *two* sets of footprints. I know you've always been desperate to prove that your fairies are lovely little creatures, but I seem to remember that they were a bit sneaky.'

She shrugs and says, 'And I seem to remember that your stupid ninjabread men came in all shapes and sizes. Maybe some of them have human-shaped feet!' And with that she goes back to admiring Pebble's patchwork leaf blanket.

I suppose it's possible, but because I'm not as trusting as Rose I keep looking around the hut for evidence that this fairy isn't as sweet as she seems.

Pebble is clearly ingenious. The stove has been made from an enormous cowrie shell and fresh water is delivered to the hut through a network of bamboo canes. There are more of her pictures in here too, drawn on pieces of driftwood. Mainly they are of birds and fish, but there is one picture of a person. It's on her shelf of special things and it shows a stick figure with a round face and sticking up hair. It could be anyone, really – it could even be Pebble herself – but there's something sitting next to the picture that makes the hairs on my arms prickle.

It's a single black feather.

I reach out, but before I can touch it Pebble's hand snatches it away. She hides it in her fist, a look of fear on her face, and the next thing I know we're being pushed out of the hut and back into the bright sunshine. Our tour is over.

Pebble stomps ahead of us, leading us back to the beach. As we go, Win insists on doing his super-stealthy walk, creeping from tree to tree, and looking out for any sign of the ninjabread men. I stare into the shadowy trees too, but I'm not looking for biscuity faces covered in hoods. I'm seeing if I can spot a pale sack face or black wings, and I'm listening for the crackle of straw . . .

Win and I soon discover that it's hard to be hyper-vigilant when you're walking with a fairy who's making bird sounds. Pebble twits and whistles as she walks along and birds of all sizes start to swoop down from the canopy and fly over our heads.

'Pebble, any chance you could stop doing that?' I say, when a large parrot almost flies into my face.

'Leave her alone, Arthur,' says Rose. 'The birds are cool!' But I do notice she wraps her hands round her dragon's egg.

Soon we reach the beach and the birds fly away. Mitch is clearly keen to get going and has pulled the rowing boat back into the water. 'Come on,' she says. 'We've still got two more islands to visit.'

Win, Rose and I stand in the shade of a tree to say goodbye to Pebble.

'Why don't you come with us?' says Rose.

Pebble glances at the sea and at the dark shape of the *Alisha*.

'We're going to visit more islands then sail back to Roar,' continues Rose. 'Win and Mitch live there. They'll look after you.'

But something about what Rose has said makes Pebble shake her head wildly. She backs away from the sea, and I wonder if she's scared of water after travelling all the way here in her small rowing boat.

'Look,' I say, pointing at *Alisha*. 'Our boat is huge. You'll be safe on there.'

But she just frowns and digs her feet into the sand and we soon realise that Pebble is never going to come with us.

After hugs all round – which hurt because Pebble is so strong – we get ready to leave.

'I'm pleased that we found you,' says Rose. 'I always told Arthur that you were awesome.'

And at that moment something strange happens.

We hear a voice coming from the trees above us. A whispery voice that says, '*Streeeeeetch . . .*' Pebble grins and claps her hands with barely contained glee.

'*Streeeeeetch,*' comes the voice again, only louder this time. 'You've got to *streeeeetch,* Rose Trout!'

CHAPTER 21

We look up. Perched in the branches of the tree is an old lady. She's got short grey hair, thin arms and legs, and she's wearing a bright blue leotard. Her eyes are a similarly dazzling shade of blue and they glitter mischievously.

'*Bendy Joan?*' says Rose.

The old lady grins. 'Yes . . . That's me!' And then, in one swift motion, she gets to her feet, trots along the branch – arms outstretched – and gets ready to drop to the ground.

'RUN!' shouts Rose.

We plunge out of the shade and into the sunshine, heading towards the waiting boat. A light thud tells us that Joan has landed and we pick up speed, trying to make our legs move as fast as possible through the fine sand.

'Hurry up!' shouts Mitch. Then she starts fiddling with one of the bottles round her neck.

I glance back and see Joan cartwheeling towards us. She stops, stretches her arms up to the sky, and then starts to backflip instead. Her backflips are even faster than her cartwheels!

Win pulls out his wand and beats Mitch to a spell. 'Ivy dingle!' A puff of bright green smoke explodes from his wand and . . . that's it. The smoke confuses Joan, but only for a moment.

'Come on,' I say, dragging Win forward.

I can hear Joan's panting breath, and something else: giggles! I glance back and see that Pebble is running alongside Joan and laughing hysterically.

I told Rose the fairies were sneaky!

We reach the sea just as Mitch throws her spell into the air. 'Get in!' she shouts, and we haul ourselves into the rowing boat. Moments later a powerful wave roars past us, lifting the rowing boat up and then down again.

I turn round in time to see the wave hit Bendy Joan and Pebble and sweep them up the beach. It dumps them on the sand. Pebble jumps up and tries to help Joan to her feet, but she shakes her off and leaps forward, launching herself into a triple roll.

'Go, Mitch!' I shout. 'GO!'

Mitch swims fast, pulling the boat behind her, and we shoot out to sea, water spraying up behind us. Shaky and out of breath, we drag ourselves on to the wooden seats.

While Rose takes out her dragon-egg stone and checks it for cracks, back on the beach Bendy Joan does an energetic gymnastics display. She seems to have forgotten about us and is now rolling a coconut along one arm, behind her head, then along her other arm. Pebble is sitting cross-legged in the sand in front of her, watching admiringly. She claps appreciatively as Joan tosses the coconut up in the air then flips into a handstand and catches it with her feet.

Rose laughs. 'At least we know who made that second set of footprints!'

'Oi, you lot!' shouts Mitch. 'Is anyone going to row?'

I grab the oars and as we move closer to the *Alisha* we relive the exciting events on Dolphin-Shark Island. Win describes his fight with the ninjabread men in vivid detail and even finds a chunk of biscuit in the hood of his robes. 'I think it's a bit of hand,' he says, then after glancing at me, he breaks it into four pieces and passes them round. Mitch's piece is tossed into the air and her hand shoots up to catch it.

'Delicious,' says Rose. 'Shame you didn't get a whole arm.'

I drag the oars through the waves. While Rose and Win crunch on their biscuits, I tell them what I saw in Pebble's hut.

'You say the person in the picture had spiky hair?' says Rose, then she points back at the beach where Bendy Joan is still cavorting. 'Joan's hair is pretty spiky, and maybe she gave Pebble the feather. It could have come from a chicken for all we know.'

I shake my head. 'You didn't see the look on her face, Rose. Pebble looked terrified when she was holding the feather, and I know exactly who makes you feel like that:

Crowky.'

'I'll tell you who else would make you feel terrified,' says Win. 'A giant chicken!'

And then they both start laughing, and when Win does an impression of a giant chicken it suddenly seems ridiculous that I thought the feather had to come from Crowky.

When Win clucks loudly in my face, I pass him the oars and decide to eat my piece of ninjabread man.

Rose is right: they do taste delicious.

CHAPTER 22

We spent longer than we planned on Dolphin-Shark Island so the moment we climb on board the *Alisha* we weigh anchor. We need to get going if we're going to visit the last two islands. Luckily for us a strong wind has picked up and soon we're racing across the water towards the distant blobs of land.

The wind is so gusty that Win and I don't fancy climbing up to the crow's nest. Instead Win goes to help the bosun who is having problems steering the ship and Mitch uses her hatch to go to her cabin. She's planning to 'consult the mushrooms', whatever that means.

Rose and I watch as Dolphin-Shark Island gets smaller.

'I wish Pebble had come with us,' says Rose.

Now that I've met Pebble I'm feeling a bit guilty that I banished the fairies. I'm not sure I ever gave them a chance.

'Rose,' I say, 'how come I didn't want your fairies in Roar? I mean, I know one of them bit me, but Pebble seemed harmless. She's just a little girl who's into animals.'

Rose laughs. 'Pebble is not *just* a little girl, Arthur. She's a real fairy and that means she's powerful.' I must look sceptical because she carries on. 'Look, I know I was furious when you got rid of my fairies, but you might have had a point. Real fairies are nothing like the tiny things you see collecting acorns in cartoons. They're incredibly strong and fast, they're vengeful too, and they each have a magical power. Oh, and they steal things.'

'But Pebble wasn't like that,' I say. 'She had a vegetable patch and those animals loved her. And she certainly didn't steal anything.'

'Oh, didn't she?' says Rose with a grin, then she pulls Win's binoculars out of her bag.

'Where did you get them?' I say, patting my pocket where I last put them. Of course it's empty.

'I watched Pebble take them out of your pocket minutes after she met you. Then, when we were in her hut, she slipped them under her pillow and that's when I took them back.'

I take the binoculars from Rose and that's when I notice red marks on my fingers. I remember how hard Pebble squeezed my hand when she pulled me through the jungle. 'If she's so powerful, then how come you asked her to come on the ship with us?' I ask.

Rose looks at me as if I'm stupid. 'She'd never hurt *us*, would she? Fairies only do bad stuff to their enemies – which, by the way, you'd know if you'd ever bothered to read the

Fairy Fact File – plus, we can take away their powers.'

'How?'

She shrugs. 'I can't remember.'

'But let me guess: it's written down in the Fairy Fact File?'

'Yep. I keep telling you that you should have read it.'

'You wrote the thing, but you can't seem to remember much of it,' I protest.

'True!' she says with a laugh.

Suddenly Mitch flings open her hatch and pulls herself on to the deck. Her eyes dart around, taking in the white-tipped waves and the bulging sails. A powerful gust of wind blows her blue hair up in the air and water sloshes over the side of her hot tub.

'I don't like this,' she says, glancing at the compass she keeps round her neck. 'Somehow we've sailed off course. I can't even see the other two islands!'

I look out to sea. Mitch is right. The islands we were sailing towards have disappeared. The *Alisha* is alone on the ocean, surrounded by endless rolling waves.

'There's something else too,' says Mitch. 'I can feel magic in the air.'

'*What?*' says Rose.

'Magic. It's prickling my skin. Can't you feel it?'

'Are you sure it's not a *storm* you're feeling in the air?' I say. The clouds are getting darker by the second. It feels like night is falling.

Mitch scowls. 'I know the smell of magic, Arthur. It smells

121

of marzipan and pears and –' she pauses here to sniff deeply – 'very old books.'

'So what do we do?' I say.

Mitch shrugs. 'Batten down the hatches and turn the ship round.'

'But what about the last two islands?' says Rose, hugging her egg to her.

Just then a flash of lightning bursts through the clouds and strikes the sea. Seconds later the thunder comes, a rumble so deep it makes my teeth shake.

'Forget about them,' says Mitch. 'We're going home.'

CHAPTER 23

The storm strikes fast. The wind whips the sea into ferocious waves and the *Alisha* is tossed from side to side.

While Win and I scramble up and down ropes to help the orangutans secure the sails, Rose takes the wheel and Mitch hurls spells over the side of the ship.

Pink, blue and black smoke pours from her hands. She makes a wind to force the storm away and then tries to freeze the waves. She pours sunlight from a bottle, but it's whipped out to sea in a flash. Nothing works, but this doesn't stop her from trying.

Win and I climb from mast to mast, struggling to pull the heavy sails in. Soon my fingers are raw from the wet ropes and I'm soaked from the waves crashing over us. We manage to secure most of them, but the biggest – the mainsail – is proving impossible. It whips round, catching one orangutan on the side of her head and sending her tumbling towards the deck. At the last second she grabs a rope, swinging to safety.

'Arthur, Win, get down from there!' shouts Mitch. 'It's too dangerous!'

Win and I climb down from the rigging and stagger over the deck to help Rose with the wheel. It's spinning wildly in her hands and it takes all three of us to get it back under control. Up on her platform Mitch keeps throwing spells into the air until the deck is thick with the smell of marzipan, pears and very old books.

But the waves keep coming – getting bigger and bigger – and the wind builds until it's impossible to do anything except try to control the wheel. The front of the ship rises up and up until we're teetering on the edge of a huge wave.

'HOLD ON!' yells Mitch.

We grab hold of whatever we can and the apes wrap their long arms round ropes. Then, with a shudder, the *Alisha* crashes down. Timbers groan and icy water washes across the deck, knocking me away from the others and dragging me towards the side of the ship. I panic, scrabbling to grab hold of something.

'Arthur!' Win hurls a rope in my direction and I catch it and pull myself back towards the wheel. The *Alisha* starts to climb another wave and that's when Rose decides to tie the three of us together. She slings the rope round us and secures it to the wheel.

Suddenly the ship tips forward and plummets down. The sea crashes over the deck again.

'Get below deck!' Mitch has to bellow to be heard over the howling wind. The apes realise there's nothing more they can do and scurry through the hatch, but the bosun won't leave Mitch. She hunkers down next to her, one long arm wrapped protectively round her tail.

'Didn't you hear me?' Mitch shouts at us. 'I said: *get below deck!*'

The *Alisha* hovers at the crest of the wave, then we're tipping forward again.

'If you're staying out here, then so are we!' yells Rose as the *Alisha* plunges down and water surges across the deck.

Suddenly Win wriggles an arm free from the rope and pulls out his wand. 'I'm going to do a spell,' he says. 'Something to help.' His hand is shaking as he points the wand towards the stormy sky and cries, 'Hairy pip!'

Rose and I look at each other in alarm. What sort of a spell is *hairy pip?*

We soon find out. A single thread flies out of his wand and whips round in the air. More threads follow. They tangle together until a thick grey blanket is flapping above us. Win grabs hold of it and pulls it round our shoulders. We huddle under it like a tent. Then, hearts thudding and bodies trembling, we watch as Mitch tries to save our ship.

She works her way through her remaining bottles until she has shaken every last drop from them. But the wind snatches away the puffs of smoke and stars before they can become ice or sunshine. With a cry of frustration Mitch

throws a last handful of dried flowers into the air. It calms the wind for a few seconds, letting Mitch wriggle her way across the deck to join us under the blanket. The bosun finally goes below deck.

'Good spell, Win,' she says, pulling the blanket round her. 'Couldn't have done better myself.'

And that's when I start to feel really scared because Mitch hardly ever says anything nice about Win's magic.

Lightning explodes from the sky. It's coming thick and fast now and the thunder is a constant growl. A flash of white strikes so close that the hairs on my arms stand on end. Then the inevitable happens.

There is a heart-stopping BANG followed by a blinding flash. The *Alisha* has been struck by lightning! Splintered wood flies in all directions and fire burns somewhere above us. Then, through the confusion of flames and smoke, the mainmast begins to topple forward . . . straight towards us! Win desperately tugs at the ropes. Rose and I help, but we're tied too tightly to the wheel. We can't escape.

Next to me Mitch smashes a bottle between her hands and throws the glass and everything left inside up into the air. Seconds before the mast hits us a gust of wind shoves it to one side. The burning wood crashes past my face and slams into the deck.

For a moment none of us speak. We stare at each other wide-eyed. Then Win manages to say, 'That was a good spell too, Mitch.'

'I know,' she says, before flopping back on the ash-covered deck and laughing wildly. The ship tips, smacking into a wave and water rolls over Mitch and then the burning mast. The fire goes out with a hiss.

'What do we do now?' says Rose. The ship is rolling from side to side, each time tipping a little further, and the sky is alive with lightning.

Mitch drags herself to the railing and stares across the sea, taking in the endless, angry waves. Then she laughs and cries out, 'I don't believe it!'

'What?' shouts Rose.

I fumble for the binoculars and then I see what's making Mitch so happy: there's a lump of land rising out of the sea. It looks solid and safe. It looks close.

'It's an island!' I say.

CHAPTER 24

We can't sail to the island because the mainmast is lying smashed across the deck, but finally luck is on our side because the storm seems to drag us forward. We untie ourselves from the wheel and join Mitch at the railing, then we watch as we drift closer to the island. Waves still crash around us, but safety is within reach. The sun even breaks through the clouds.

One by one, the orangutans come up from below deck and join us. We can see the island more clearly now. It's covered in thick jungle and has steep sides; it looks like the top of a mountain rising out of the sea.

'This weather is so strange,' says Mitch, her eyes moving from the blue sky above us to the waves. She takes out her telescope and trains it on the island. 'And that's strange too . . .'

I look through Win's binoculars. We're drifting towards a perfectly round bay. In the middle of this bay is a wide sandy beach, and winding away from the beach and up the side of the mountain is a wooden staircase. I follow it with the binoculars until it disappears into jungle.

If there are stairs, then that means someone built them. But for once I don't think of Crowky. The staircase is old: the wood is weathered and vines creep over it as if it's part of the jungle itself.

'What's that?' says Win.

He's pointing at a tower built on the rocks at the tip of the bay. It looks like it's been hollowed out of a huge tree trunk. The wind pulls the *Alisha* closer and soon we're passing in front of it. Now we can see that the top of the tower is made of entwined branches. Something bright glitters inside.

'I think it's a lighthouse!' says Rose. 'And look: someone's up there!'

Two small figures are standing on the balcony. One of them has dark hair and is reaching out towards us, eyes screwed shut. The other has fair hair and is standing just behind them.

'The one at the front is calming the storm,' I say, because that's what it looks like they're doing: using their hands to push back the wind and the rough sea. Almost as soon as the words are out of my mouth the *Alisha* slips into the sheltered bay and the wind dies away. The figure on the balcony flops forward as if they're exhausted and the little blond person jumps up and down and waves.

We wave back and laugh and yell, hardly able to believe that we're safe. Next to me, Win shouts 'Spider chew!' and a green ball of fire shoots from his wand and lights up the sky with an explosion of stars. The orangutans swing up what's left of the rigging to grunt and whoop.

Rose grabs my arm. 'I know where we are, Arthur! Do you remember what Mum used to say when we were little and it was time for us to go to bed?'

How could I forget? Mum said it every single night as we walked – or rather she dragged us – up the stairs. 'Up the wooden hill to fairyland,' I say, slipping into the sing-song voice Mum always used.

Rose points to the staircase rising up from the beach. 'Well, that staircase is made of wood – it's a wooden hill – and those two –' she turns to the tree-trunk lighthouse where the small figures are still standing – 'are fairies. Arthur, I think we've just arrived in fairyland!'

CHAPTER 25

The *Alisha* glides into the middle of the bay then comes to a gentle stop.

For a moment no one speaks. Even the orangutans are silent as we take in the still turquoise water, the blue sky and the winding staircase. We're in shock. The calm, the bright colours, the gentle air blowing over us . . . it's such a contrast to the storm we've left behind.

'What are we waiting for?' says Rose. 'Let's go and meet the rest of my fairies!'

Leaving the orangutans to examine the damage to the *Alisha*, Rose, Win and I row to shore while Mitch swims alongside us.

'Rose, are you sure this is a good idea?' I say, pulling on the oars. 'Don't you remember what you told me about fairies? How they steal and have incredible strength and secret powers?'

Rose dismisses my words with a wave of her hand. 'Fairies only do that to their enemies and those two just saved our lives. Why would they do that if they wanted to hurt us?'

She's got a point, and Pebble was definitely more cheeky than wicked, but Mitch isn't so easily convinced. Her face pops out of the sea and her eyes dart around the bay suspiciously. 'I don't like it,' she says. 'There's a real pongy smell of magic in the air.'

'Sorry, that was me!' says Win.

Mitch scowls and uses her tail to splash water in his face. 'I'm serious, Win – marzipan, pears, leathery books – even you should be able to smell it!'

'Of course you can smell magic,' says Rose. 'They're fairies, so they're magical. Plus they just used their amazing magic to stop a storm and save our lives. I don't know who it was waving their hands around on the balcony, but I'm sure one of my fairies could calm storms . . . or maybe they could make them?'

'I still don't like it,' says Mitch firmly. Then she scowls and dives under the water with a flick of her strong tail.

'She's just annoyed that it wasn't her magic that saved us,' whispers Win.

Suddenly a fish shoots out of the sea and hits Win in the face. It's accompanied by pink fizzing stars. 'Wow!' says Win. 'She can hear *and* do magic underwater!'

Soon our rowing boat hits sand and Mitch reappears to watch as we heave it out of the water. She doesn't offer to help, even though she's stronger than all three of us put together. She just floats in the water, arms folded, her eyes taking in the beach and the jungle behind.

'There is one thing you should probably know about fairies,' says Rose as we pull the boat higher up the beach.

'What's that?' I say.

'They can enchant you,' says Rose.

'What does that mean exactly?' I say.

'Oh, you know,' Rose says, waving her hands around vaguely. 'They can make you fall under their spell. That kind of thing.'

The flight of wooden stairs is directly in front of us. We can see buildings hidden among the trees too. Actually, they're more like tree houses because they're made of wood and seem to grow out of the trees themselves.

'How do we stop ourselves from becoming enchanted?' I ask.

But Rose is distracted. One of the fairies has burst on to the beach and is running across the sand towards us. Well, I say running, but I'm not sure if there's a word to describe what the fairy is doing. It's sprinting so fast it's a blur of legs and arms.

Win laughs. 'That is one fast fairy!'

Skidding to a stop we see that it's one of the figures from the lighthouse. A girl.

'Rose and Arthur Trout!' she cries. 'It's you, isn't it? I recognised you immediately. Welcome! Oh my goodness, this is amazing. You're here . . . You're actually *here*! I'm so happy I could scream!' And then she does scream:

a high-pitched, spine-tingling sound that's so painful I have to cover my ears.

Rose laughs. '*Moss?* Is that you?'

The fairy stares up at us with the biggest, greenest eyes I've ever seen. 'YES!' she cries, jumping up and down in the sand. 'It's me! It's really me, and you are *here!*'

Unlike her sister, Moss has no problem talking. She dances around on the sand as she gabbles away about the storm and the amazing fact that we're here on the island. She doesn't pause for breath, which means I can get a good look at her. She comes up to Rose's waist and she has messy white-blonde hair with feathers, shells and possibly a bee tangled in it. Her smile is big and friendly and only slightly ruined by her sharp teeth. She's wearing some sort of leafy-dress thing. If I'm honest, she looks a bit like she's fallen out of a tree and hit every branch on the way down.

'Let me help you with that,' she says, then she picks the boat up from where we dropped it in the sand, and I mean she literally picks it up and holds it over her head. The rowing boat is heavy. Three of us were struggling to drag it up the beach, but Moss carries it up the beach and chucks it down in the sand.

'Whoa . . .' says Win.

'Rose!' I say, grabbing her before she can run after Moss. 'You never said how we can avoid being enchanted. Quick. Tell me now!'

'Oh, I can't really remember,' she says, frowning. 'Don't

take presents from them? No, that wasn't it . . . Maybe we're not supposed to accept food off them? Look, it doesn't matter, Arthur. They won't enchant us. We're their friends!' And with that she runs across the sand to carry on talking to Moss.

'Did you hear that, Win?' I say. 'Just in case, don't accept any presents or food from the fairies.'

'What's that?' he says, his voice muffled.

When I turn round I see that he's crunching down on a big juicy apple. 'Win! Where did you get that?'

He nods to his left. 'This little guy gave it to me.'

And that's when I notice another fairy has joined us. He's standing next to Win and he's as dark as Moss is fair.

'I've got one for you, Arthur!'

This voice comes from right beside me. I look down to see a third fairy smiling at me and I'm sure this is the one who stopped the storm. He looks similar to the fairy standing by Win, only he has freckles and his black hair is even wilder. In his outstretched hand he holds a perfect red apple. It gleams in the sun and suddenly I realise just how hungry and thirsty I am. 'How do you feel, Win?' I say. 'Any weird side effects from eating that apple?'

'Nah,' he says. 'I feel totally and utterly normal.'

I'm not convinced Win knows what normal feels like, so as politely as possible I shake my head and say, 'I'm not hungry, thanks.'

The fairy shrugs and bites into it himself, his sharp teeth

slicing through the white flesh. 'I'm Owl,' he says, juice running down his chin. 'I'm the one with freckles and brown eyes.' He stares hard at me to prove his point. 'My brother's got no freckles, blue eyes and a funny bit on his ear.'

'Was that you on the lighthouse just then?' I ask, and Owl nods eagerly. 'You calmed the storm for us, didn't you?'

His eyes grow a little bit bigger and he presses a finger to his lips.

Win nudges me. 'He can't tell you, Arthur. Remember their special magical powers are a secret.'

'I know, but we saw him do it.'

'Rules are rules,' says Win with a shrug.

Suddenly Win is shoved to one side and the other fairy, Owl's brother, plants himself in front of me. 'I'm Twig!' he says.

'And that's the lot of us,' says Moss. 'Twig, Owl and me.' Then she turns, takes Rose by the hand and pulls her towards the wooden hill.

Twig's fingers wrap round mine. 'Come on,' he says, dragging me across the sand. 'We've got slides!'

CHAPTER 26

We allow ourselves to be led up the staircase and on to a covered platform overlooking the bay. There are cushions everywhere and a cool breeze blows off the sea.

'Sit down! Sit down!' says Moss, zipping around and plumping up cushions. 'You must be tired after that storm. It was massive. Just gigantic. One of the biggest I've ever seen!'

Again I ask if it was Owl's special powers that stopped the storm. The three fairies look at each other and grin, but refuse to admit that Owl did anything.

After a moment's silence Rose says, 'Well . . . thank you anyway. It was amazing, *you're* amazing, and now we have to tell you who we met today.'

The fairies stare up at her, still smiling.

'Pebble!' says Rose.

Instantly the fairies' smiles disappear. Moss gasps and grabs hold of her brothers' hands. 'You found Pebble?' she says, worry written across her face. 'Did she say what happened to her?'

'She didn't say a word,' says Rose, 'but she used to talk, didn't she?'

'Lots and lots,' says Moss, brightening for a moment, but then she sighs deeply. 'Poor Pebble. She got scared of the ghost so she took our little boat and sailed away. We told her not to, didn't we?' Owl and Twig nod in unison. 'You see, the sea outside the bay is stormy all the time and too rough for little boats, but she was so scared she didn't listen to us and ran away.'

'Well you don't need to worry about her any more because she's safe,' says Rose, and she goes on to describe Pebble's home on Dolphin-Shark Island and her unusual friend Bendy Joan. The fairies listen intently, nodding and encouraging her to say more. Every now and then they share wide-eyed looks, like when they hear about her vegetable patch and the fact that their boat is now a roof on her hut.

'And,' says Win, raising his head from a particularly squishy cushion, 'she's sharing the island with an army of lethal ninjabread men that I destroyed with my ninja skills!'

'Don't worry,' I say quickly. 'They're made of biscuit and they're small. They won't hurt Pebble.'

'It was extremely tough biscuit,' mutters Win, but he seems too tired to argue with me.

Owl sighs and says, 'I miss Pebble!'

Twig blows his curly hair out of his eyes. 'Me too.'

'Hang on,' I say, struggling to sit up. 'What do you mean, *she got scared of the ghost?*'

'Oh, we'll tell you about that later,' says Moss. 'Now, do you want cake? It's still warm and it's got coconut in it!'

She runs off at her usual breakneck speed and comes back seconds later with a big cinnamon-and-coconut-scented cake. Rose takes one look at it and announces that she was definitely wrong about the whole accepting-food-from-fairies thing. And when Twig offers us some of his 'choc 'n' nut 'n' cherry cookies', even I agree that there's no way food that looks this good could ever do us any harm.

While we eat, the fairies tell us about their life. 'We've been here for ever,' says Moss. 'Just the four of us – well, until Pebble went. We love it!'

I shoot a quick look at Rose. I've been wondering if the fairies remember that it was me who sent them away to The End. If they do, they're either too polite to mention it or it really doesn't bother them. Instead they chatter on and on about their 'amazing island' with its waterfalls, swings, caves and slides. Twig and Owl are desperate to give us a tour, but right now we're too tired after the storm and too full of cake to move.

From where I'm lying, covered in crumbs, I can look down from the platform and see the whole of the bay: the *Alisha* bobbing on blue glittering water, the jungle that creeps down to the beach and, at the tip of the cove, Moss's lighthouse.

Because it's clearly *her* lighthouse. She keeps telling us.

'Do you like my lighthouse? I made it. The others didn't

141

help me at all. I built it all on my own so I could help big boats like yours. We *love* big boats –' Twig and Owl nod their heads in agreement – 'and then you came along, which means my lighthouse worked and I helped a big boat!' Moss takes a deep breath and beams at us. She can talk as fast as she can run.

The fairies are all clearly obsessed with the *Alisha*. They keep jumping up to look at it through a telescope and chattering about lending us tools and helping us mend the mast.

'We're good at making things,' says Owl.

'Except big boats,' says Twig, and all three fairies shake their heads sadly. 'We tried, and we made one that was quite good but it got smashed up by the waves like all the others.'

'It was soooooo scary!' says Owl, his eyes as big as, well, an owl. 'Even Moss was scared.'

Moss does not like this. 'Shut up!' she says, giving him a shove that sends him flying across the cushions. 'I was not!'

Twig grins. 'Yes you were, and you cried when it fell apart and we had to swim back to the island!'

In a flash Moss leaps up and launches herself at Twig. She's smaller than him, but even so she manages to pin

him to the floor. 'I got SEA in my eyes! That's what it was, Twig. Sea. SEA!'

'Yes, sorry, Moss. It was definitely sea,' says Twig, which is exactly what I would have said if Moss was pinning me to the ground and baring her teeth.

Moss jumps off him and smiles sweetly at us. 'Now we're going to help you mend your boat.'

After a quick conversation the three fairies disappear into the jungle to find 'a massive tree'. The platform seems strangely quiet with them gone.

Rose yawns and stretches her arms above her head. 'We should probably go and help . . .'

'We'd only get in the way,' says Win, taking another cookie.

For a moment we lie on our cushions in happy silence. 'I told you we should never have sent them to The End,' says Rose.

Flower-perfumed air drifts over me and birds call to each other from the trees. After the wild panic of the storm, this feels like heaven.

'You're right,' I say, reaching for another slice of coconut cake. 'And they can really bake.'

CHAPTER 27

When I wake up, my mind feels muddled, and for a moment I don't know where I am, but then I see a wooden balcony and rainbow stars twinkling over a bay and I remember that I'm on the fairies' island. I grope around on the floor until I find the telescope and then I look out to sea. All seems peaceful on the *Alisha*. I can see a couple of orangutans sitting on the ropes and there is a light on in Mitch's cabin.

Mitch.

Rose and Win must have nodded off too because they're lying asleep next to me. I shake Rose awake.

'What's the matter?' she says, struggling to sit up.

'We fell asleep and forgot about Mitch. We came up here, stuffed our faces with cake and left Mitch on the beach!'

Win sits up and shivers. He pulls his ninja robes round him. 'She is not going to like that,' he says.

'And there's another thing,' I say, holding up the telescope. 'This is *Mitch's* telescope. The fairies must have stolen it from her. They were using it right in front of us and we didn't even notice!'

I hear something behind me and spin round.

Moss is standing there twisting her fingers and gazing up at me. 'I'm sorry. That was me. I took it.' My heart thuds from the shock of seeing her there. 'I didn't think it was stealing. We share everything here.'

I feel embarrassed. The fairies have been incredibly kind to us and I've just accused them of pinching our stuff.

'We're just worried about our friend, Mitch,' says Rose. 'She's the mermaid and it's her telescope. Have you seen her?'

Moss nods. 'She was swimming in the bay, then she made a fire with her hands, then she said, "What are you staring at?" and then she went back to the big boat.'

That sounds like Mitch.

'I should go and see her,' says Rose. 'Check that she's OK.'

She heads towards the wooden staircase, but Owl gasps and leaps forward, blocking her way. Where did he come from? 'Not now!' he says. 'It's not safe for you to go wandering around at night because of the ghost.'

The ghost again. 'What do you mean?' I say.

Owl looks up at me through his messy fringe. 'We've got a ghost,' he says seriously. 'It lives in the middle of the island, but sometimes at night it comes over here.'

'What does it look like?' says Rose suspiciously.

Moss zips forward and pushes Owl out of the way. '*Horrible!*' she says. 'I mean, we've never properly seen it, but we've definitely got one and it's wicked and spooky and mean.'

'Hang on,' I say. 'If you've never properly seen it, how do you know you've got one?'

'Because once I saw its *staring eyes!*' It's Twig who says this. He's sitting on the edge of the balcony swinging his legs. I wish the fairies would stop appearing out of thin air. They're making me jump more than any ghost could.

'And I saw this shadow flying around,' adds Owl.

Flying around? I don't like the sound of that. 'When exactly did your ghost appear?' I ask. We left Crowky floating in the sea six months ago . . . Could he possibly have flown all the way here? As the fairies gather in a huddle to discuss their ghost I'm willing them to say it came years ago or that it's always been here.

'We think,' says Moss, 'that it was around seventeen quarter moons ago, give or take the odd star day.'

What? I decide to try a different approach. 'How many days is it since your ghost arrived?'

'Seventeen!' says Twig.

Owl scoffs. 'No it wasn't. It was seventeen hundreds!'

'You idiots!' says Moss. 'It was seventy-seven seven-two. Anyway, you don't need to worry because the ghost only comes out at night. It's fine during the day. Go and see your friend in the morning!'

And with that the fairies disappear again. I mean, they don't actually disappear, they just run away really fast, calling out, 'Night night, Arthur! See you tomorrow, Rose! Bye, Win!'

I join Rose and Win at the edge of the platform . We look out over the quiet bay. We can hear the swoosh of the waves and leaves rustling in the wind. We glance at the trees that surround us, and I know that we're all looking for the 'shadow' and the 'staring eyes' that the fairies mentioned.

A green parrot flies through the trees and perches on the edge of the balcony. It puffs up its feathers, scratches its pink beak with a claw then stares at us. We take a step closer together.

'Ghosts don't exist,' says Rose firmly, 'but it is very dark and you know my feelings about that . . . Tomorrow we'll make sure Mitch is OK and get the boat fixed. Then we'll go home.'

Home. Whether it's Win's cave, Mitch's island or Grandad's house – right now, they all seem very far away. The parrot whistles, making us jump.

'Bedtime?' says Win.

Sleep seems like a much better idea than ghost-watching so we make beds out of the cushions on the floor and a pile of blankets the fairies have left for us. Incredibly they've even put out a tray containing mugs of warm juice and a plate of cookies.

I eat my cookies snuggled down under a blanket, trying and failing to keep the crumbs out. Almost immediately I feel better, safer. Plus the parrot is still on the balcony and

it's making gentle whistling sounds . . . Perhaps it's snoring
. . . Do parrots snore?

'Hey, Arthur,' whispers Rose. 'You do realise that we've
gone up the wooden hill to fairyland and now we're falling
asleep. How cool is that?'

Very, I think, as once again I drift into a deep, cake-filled
sleep.

CHAPTER 28

We wake to sunshine and the smell of the sea. This morning the idea of a ghost on this island seems ridiculous, especially when Moss appears and announces that she's made banana pancakes for breakfast.

Rose insists that we take the pancakes down to the beach so we can have them with Mitch, but when we get down there she's nowhere to be seen. It's only when we've almost finished breakfast that she rolls up on the beach with a wave.

'Hello,' she says, wringing water out of her hair then tossing it over her shoulder. 'What are you lot doing?'

'Having breakfast,' says Win. 'Do you want some?'

She wrinkles up her nose at the sight of the pancakes. 'No thanks. I've already eaten.'

Rose goes and sits with her at the edge of the waves. She gives her the telescope back, puts her arm round her, and then she says something that makes Mitch laugh. It doesn't take much for Mitch to forgive Rose.

I notice that the fairies are watching Mitch closely, gazing at her tail as it flips around in the water and at the colourful tattoos that cover her skin. I guess she's the first heavily tattooed mermaid they've ever seen. Suddenly Moss jumps to her feet and shouts, 'Hey, mermaid! Would you like a house down here on the beach?'

Mitch looks taken aback. 'Oh, I'm OK on the *Alisha*, thanks.'

Moss shrugs like it's no big deal, then says. 'We'll make you one anyway in case you change your mind. Twig, come on. Make her a house!'

Obediently Twig stuffs the rest of his pancake in his mouth and trots over to Moss. They have a quick conversation, then Twig scampers into the jungle and comes back with an armful of tree trunks, branches and vines. He dumps it on the sand, close to the water's edge, then Moss says, 'Go on. Do it, Twig!'

What happens next is incredible.

With Moss watching carefully and giving instructions Twig sets to work. He moves so fast it's like watching a film on fast-forward. He sticks the branches and tree trunks into the sand and twists vines round them. Then, when he's made a rough hut shape, he stands back to assess his work. Moss marches forward and rearranges a few vines.

'It's a bit holey,' Win whispers to me.

But Twig hasn't finished. Next he stretches his hands out – just like Owl stretched his fingers out when he was calming the storm – then he closes his eyes and starts wriggling his fingers.

Win nudges me. 'What's he up to?'

What he's up to is magic. The air fills with the smell of pears and marzipan and as Twig wiggles his fingers faster and faster the vines and branches burst into life. They start to grow, sending out shoots that twist round each other in complicated patterns. Twig lifts one hand and a roof springs into place. With a swish of his fingers windows appear. In under a minute Twig's holey hut has become a home with a leafy roof. It sits at the very edge of the sand, where the beach meets the sea, so that the foamy waves can roll in through the door and then out again, keeping it cool and wet. It's perfect for Mitch.

Twig brushes his hands and grins at us. 'There it is. I made a mermaid house!'

So his magical power is making twigs grow. I suppose the clue was in his name.

'Now do you want us to mend your boat?' asks Moss.

'No, thanks,' says Mitch, refusing to be impressed with her twiggy house.

'Yes we do!' I say.

Mitch rolls her eyes. 'We can mend the boat on our own, Arthur. I can do magic too, remember?'

Rose puts her hand on Mitch's shoulder. 'We know you can, Mitch, but it's a matter of time. Grandad's expecting us home soon and we don't know how long it's going to take us to sail back to Roar.'

'Fine!' she snaps, but before she's had time to slam her tail down in the sea, Owl and Twig have picked up the rowing boat and dropped it in the water. Moss disappears into the forest then comes back with a tree tucked under her arm. She slings a rope round it, chucks it in the sea, then jumps in the boat and starts rowing. She shoots towards the *Alisha*, dragging the tree along behind her.

Mitch watches her go through narrowed eyes, then she uncorks a bottle, tips some green fizzing liquid on to her hand and blows it in the direction of the rowing boat. A gust of wind appears out of nowhere; it slams into the boat, making Moss fall backwards with a yelp.

Owl and Twig gasp and Rose cries, 'Mitch!'

'What?' she says with a grin. 'I was *helping*. She'll get there quicker. Now, if you don't mind, I'm going to go and keep an eye on that fairy you've invited on to my ship.'

She dives into the waves, leaving us with Owl and Twig. They grin and their pointed teeth sparkle in the sun.

'We're taking you on a tour,' says Owl.

'But only round the edge of the island,' adds Twig.

'Because of the ghost!' they say together, and then turn and run up the wooden hill.

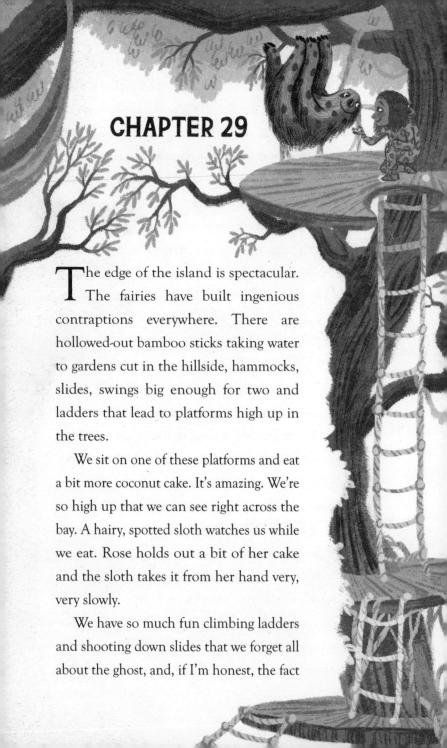

CHAPTER 29

The edge of the island is spectacular. The fairies have built ingenious contraptions everywhere. There are hollowed-out bamboo sticks taking water to gardens cut in the hillside, hammocks, slides, swings big enough for two and ladders that lead to platforms high up in the trees.

We sit on one of these platforms and eat a bit more coconut cake. It's amazing. We're so high up that we can see right across the bay. A hairy, spotted sloth watches us while we eat. Rose holds out a bit of her cake and the sloth takes it from her hand very, very slowly.

We have so much fun climbing ladders and shooting down slides that we forget all about the ghost, and, if I'm honest, the fact

that we need to leave the island at all. It's like we've washed ashore on a giant adventure playground.

'Come on! Come on!' shout Owl and Twig as they charge ahead of us. We're back on the wooden staircase that rises steeply through the jungle. The fairies have told us that it stops at 'the edge', whatever that is, and that's where they're taking us.

They climb the staircase much faster than us and when we reach the top we find them waiting for us. 'Come and look at this,' says Owl, beckoning us forward.

When we join them we get a surprise. We thought the wooden staircase was taking us to the top of the mountain and that we'd look down on the other side of the island, but

155

we're actually staring into a valley of dense jungle.

'It's like a crater,' says Rose.

I know what she means – the valley is round, but it isn't filled with rocky earth. It's green and lush and full of life. Birds rise and fall out of the canopy of leaves and their cries are loud and raucous. We can see monkeys too, and a river that must spring up somewhere in the middle of the hollow and then wriggle its way towards the sea.

'We call it the Bowl,' say Moss.

'The orangutans would love it in there,' says Win.

'No they wouldn't,' says Twig, 'because *that's* where the ghost lives and that's why we're not allowed down there.'

'Look, you two,' says Rose, using her most reasonable voice, 'there are no such things as ghosts.'

'There are and we know because Pebble got a bit of it!' The words fly out of Owl's mouth.

Twig shoves him, making him wobble on the rocky edge. 'Owl, *shut up!*' he says. 'Moss said we're not allowed to talk about that!'

'What do you mean?' I say. 'What *bit* did Pebble get?'

Owl looks over his shoulder then drops his voice to a whisper. 'Before she went away, Pebble saw the ghost. She saw it properly, but we didn't believe her so she stole a bit of it to show us. She said it came off its wing!'

His words make me feel dizzy and immediately I remember what I found in Pebble's hut. 'You mean . . . *a feather?*' I say.

156

But Owl has clamped his mouth shut and refuses to say another word.

'You can tell us,' says Rose encouragingly.

Again Owl looks around. 'We're not allowed!' His words are so quiet they're drowned out by the howl of a monkey. I glance down at the thick jungle that fills the Bowl. Anything, or anyone, could be hiding down there and we would never know.

'I think we should go back,' I say. 'We need to see if Moss has mended the boat.'

We need to get out of here is what I'm actually thinking, and Rose and Win must agree with me because the three of us run down that hill almost as fast as Owl and Twig.

Back on the beach, there's no sign of Moss, but we find Mitch inside her twig house.

She leans out of the window, glances at Owl and Twig, and then says, 'Moss has gone to her lighthouse. She said these two need to make us snacks.'

Owl and Twig don't need telling twice. They shoot off arguing about what to put inside our sandwiches: jam, honey, banana or 'everything'.

'Well, don't just stand there,' Mitch says. 'Come inside. Check out what it feels like to have the sea *inside* your house!'

It's a bit of a squeeze, and wet, but it feels good to be out of the heat of the sun and to be just the four of us again.

'Good news,' says Mitch. 'The *Alisha* is almost mended. Moss might be the biggest show-off in the world, but she

157

can do woodwork faster than anyone I know.'

'Did she use her magical power?' I ask. This is something I've been wondering about ever since we saw Twig make this house. Twig grows twigs, Owl can calm the wind and Pebble is some sort of crab whisperer, but what can Moss do?

'No,' says Mitch. 'She used the usual hammer and nails and her super fairy strength. I wanted to find out too so I tried to keep my eyes on her, but she kept shooting up to the crow's nest and disappearing below deck. You know how fast she is.' A wave rushes in through the door, bubbles over our legs then sweeps out again, leaving seaweed and a yellow crab behind.

I pick it up and let it crawl over my hand. 'Are you sure you can't remember what she can do, Rose?'

She thinks for a moment. 'No, sorry . . . It was a long time ago and everything is jumbled up from back then.'

I know what she means. Although Rose can't mention this in front of Mitch and Win, we played so many games in Grandad's attic it's hard to remember which one led to Mitch, Win and the fairies appearing. They're all mixed up together.

'I bet it's to do with her teeth,' says Mitch with a smile. 'Has anyone else noticed that they're sharper than Twig's and Owl's?'

'Yes,' says Win, 'and they're bigger too!'

I hadn't noticed, but I'm going to have a good look next time I see Moss. All this teeth talk is making me keener than ever to leave the island. 'So is the *Alisha* ready to sail?' I ask.

'The new mast is in place,' says Mitch, 'but Moss says Twig needs to do his freaky fingers thing to attach it to the deck. Apparently we'll be able to leave tomorrow.'

'Tomorrow?' I say, wishing it could be sooner.

Mitch shrugs. 'The wood needs time to "set", whatever that means.' We must look disappointed because she adds, 'What's up with you lot? I thought you loved it here!'

We shift uncomfortably in the little hut. Another wave rolls in and then out again. I put the crab down on the sand and tell Mitch what Moss and Owl said about the ghost, and how Pebble managed to get a 'bit of it'.

'And remember how Arthur saw that black feather in Pebble's hut?' adds Rose.

'You seriously think Crowky is here, on this island?' says Mitch with a smile. 'You're reading way too much into a black feather and a spooky story, but I agree that we need to get out of here. This place is weird, and I'll tell you who's weirdest of all: Moss.'

'She just mended our boat!' protests Rose.

Mitch just shakes her head impatiently. 'You can't see it, Rose, but I've got a funny feeling about her, and so have the orangutans. She makes them jittery.'

For a moment none of us talk. I'm pretty sure Mitch's 'funny feeling' comes from jealousy. Rose clearly loves hanging out with the fairies, but Mitch usually has my sister all to herself. Plus Mitch has always done the most powerful magic, then along comes this fairy with more magic in her little finger than Mitch has in her entire tail . . . It's no wonder she's not keen on her.

Rose must be thinking the same thing because she nudges Mitch and says, 'First thing tomorrow, we're leaving.'

'On our own?' says Mitch.

Rose nods. 'On our own. I asked Moss if they wanted to come with us, but she looked at me like I was mad. I suppose it is pretty nice here, even with a ghost.'

Mitch visibly sags with relief, and, to be honest, so do I. The fairies have been kind, but I'm not sure I'd like them on board the *Alisha*, popping up all over the place and annoying Mitch.

'Hello!' Moss's face appears at the window. She's grinning with excitement and jumping up and down. Mitch is right: her teeth *are* very sharp. 'I just made a *MASSIVE* banana cake to celebrate mending your big boat,' she says. 'Who wants some?'

CHAPTER 30

That evening is almost a rerun of the night before: we sit around on a big pile of cushions and eat way too much cake. Once again Mitch is missing. We told her that we could all hang out on the beach, but she said (pointedly) that she'd rather stay on the *Alisha* with a bunch of smelly orangutans.

The fairies chatter away, describing how they turned this once deserted island into their home.

'We made the staircase all on our own,' says Moss proudly. 'And the platforms and all the slides and swings.'

'I did most of them,' says Twig, wriggling his magical fingers in the air.

'No you did NOT!' says Moss. 'Anyway, shut up, Twig. We're not allowed to talk about our magic!'

'Really?' I say, because suddenly I'm desperate to know what Moss's magical power could be. 'I mean, we already know what Owl and Twig can do because we've seen them do it. Can't you give us a hint, Moss? Or a demonstration?'

Moss giggles. Her teeth glitter in the light of the setting sun. 'OK . . . Guess what? You've already seen me do it!'

Her revelation leads to me, Rose and Win trying to guess what it is that she can do.

'Excellent cake-making?' suggests Rose.

'Fast running?' I say.

'Extreme bossiness?' says Win bravely.

'No, no and no!' cries Moss, delighted. 'You don't know and I'm never, ever going to tell you!'

Twig and Owl refuse to give us any more clues, so in the end we give up and Win demonstrates his magic instead.

'I've not got one magical skill,' he says, getting out his wand and giving it a swish through the air. 'I've got, like, a million.' Then he bellows, 'Whistle fur!' and marshmallows scatter across the balcony.

It's fair to say Win's spell blows the fairies' minds.

'What is this stuff?' says Owl, stuffing four marshmallows into his mouth at once. 'You've got to make us *hundreds* before you go!'

And so Win does make more . . . and more . . . and more . . . until the platform is overflowing with marshmallows. We stuff as many as we can into jars for the fairies then eat the leftovers. We're having so much fun that it gets dark without us realising it.

The next time I glance into the jungle I see that we're surrounded by dark trees. Insects and birds call out from the shadows and I can hear strange rustling sounds. That's when I start to think about the ghost. No. That's not true. That's when I start to think about Crowky.

When I notice Rose yawning, I whisper, 'Maybe we should go and sleep on the *Alisha*?'

'NO!' cry the fairies in unison. Their hearing must be as good as their running.

Moss darts over and grabs my hand. 'You promised you'd sleep here tonight,' she says. 'You're the only visitors we've ever had and you're going tomorrow!'

I'm learning that it's hard to say no to someone with enormous eyes.

'Please stay,' says Twig, taking my other hand.

'Yes, *pleeeeease*, Arthur!' adds Owl, and he wraps his arms tight round my legs. I'm not sure I could leave even if I wanted to, plus they're right: it is only for one night.

'OK, OK,' I say. 'We'll stay here, but we've got to leave first thing in the morning.'

The fairies are so excited they decide to sleep on the balcony with us.

'Cool,' says Rose. 'It will be a sleepover!'

'YES!' says Moss, clapping her hands. 'Now it's your turn to tell us things. Tell us about Roar.'

I share a glance with Rose, wondering if the fairies can remember much about the few days they spent in Roar before I banished them. I guess they can't, because Twig fixes his big eyes on me and says, 'Yes, tell us about it. We only know about here!'

163

Rose shrugs. 'Why don't you show them the map?'

So I take out the map and the fairies 'oooh' and 'aah' over the tiny pictures of furries, unicorns and merfolk.

'Look, there's my cave,' says Win proudly, 'and behind that waterfall is the tunnel that leads to Home.'

'And what are *they*?' asks Moss, her eyes wide.

'Dragons!' says Rose, laughing.

Moss stares at the dragons Rose drew on the map years ago. 'And are they really that big?'

'Yes,' says Rose, 'and they can breathe fire too!'

Moss squeals with excitement. 'And they've got lots of teeth!'

Win goes back to the map and continues to give the fairies a tour of Roar. 'That island in the Archie Playgo is where I single-handedly took down a monkey with a bad attitude – he stole my toast. Oh, and you see that big tree by my cave? Once I karate-chopped it and a *rabbit* fell out!'

The fairies are absolutely fascinated by everything. Moss asks endless questions and soon I find myself yawning. It's late.

'What's that?' asks Moss, pointing at the Crow's Nest.

'Just a castle,' I say.

Rose must realise that I don't want to talk about Crowky because she takes the map off me and slips it in her pocket. 'We should go to sleep. We've got a long day tomorrow.'

'Definitely,' says Moss, and then she trots around the platform, bossing everyone around until six cushion beds have been set up on the floor.

As we settle down and the sounds of the jungle ring out around us, I'm pleased that the fairies have decided to sleep here with us. Lying here in the dark I can't stop my mind from drifting back to Twig and Owl's story of the ghost and his feather. The fairies might be little, but I've seen just how strong they are. It feels good to have them close by.

'Night, Arthur. Night, Rose. Night, Win,' says Owl . . . or maybe it's Twig.

CHAPTER 31

A screeching sound wakes me up.

I lie very still wondering what I just heard. Could it have been an owl or a fox? Does this island even have owls or foxes? Just as I start to think about the ghost, I hear the sound again.

This time it's more of a scream, and it's so human that I sit up and look around. In the light of the moon I can see Rose, Win, Owl and Twig lying asleep on the cushions, but Moss has gone. Could she have made the noise? Has something happened to her?

I'm about to wake up Rose when something stops me. Rose is always joking about how scared I am of everything. What if I did hear a fox, or if Moss went to get something, ran too fast and yelped? I decide to have a look around before I do or say anything.

I step over the others and head down the wooden hill. Everything is quiet and still. 'Moss?' I call out. 'Was that you?'

There's no reply so I keep going down. The air is cool, but the steps under my bare feet are still warm from the sun. The sounds of the jungle surround me and I start to wonder if it was a parrot that I heard.

The moon lights my way and soon my feet are sinking into the sand on the beach. I stand as still as possible, listening. The sea is black and the waves are gentle. Water rushes towards me and then disappears with a sigh. The light from Moss's lighthouse falls over me then swoops away across the sea.

Again I call out, 'Moss!'

Silence.

A movement at the lighthouse catches my eye. Someone is creeping along the balcony. *Is that Moss?* My heart pounds as I walk along the beach, trying to get a better look. Then I see something that makes me gasp and dig my toes into the wet sand.

The figure has wings.

I open my mouth, ready to shout for the others, but before I can do anything I hear pattering footsteps. Someone is running towards me.

Moss slams into me and grabs hold of my T-shirt. 'Arthur! Is that you?' She stares up at me with frightened eyes. 'Did you see it? I forgot to turn on the light on my lighthouse so I went out there, all on my own, and then the ghost tried to get me!'

'I saw it,' I say. 'It's still there!'

The thing up on the lighthouse has climbed on to the twiggy railing and is crouched there, wings outstretched. Suddenly it leaps into the air and glides across the sea.

Moss yelps and starts to run towards the wooden hill, dragging me along behind her. 'The ghost!' she shouts. 'The ghost! We saw the ghost!'

***

'It wasn't a ghost,' I say.

Moss and I are sitting on the platform surrounded by the others.

'It was!' insists Moss. 'It had wings, just like Twig said, and a horrible white face and spiky hair and –'

'It was Crowky,' I say, interrupting her.

Rose stares at me. 'Arthur, are you sure? We left him miles and miles away. How could he have got here?'

'I don't know, Rose, but it was definitely him!'

For a moment there is silence as Rose takes in this news. Then Moss looks up at me through her messy hair and says, 'Who is Crowky?'

I glance into the jungle then drop my voice to a whisper. 'You know that castle on our map, the Crow's Nest? Well, Crowky used to live there. He's a scarecrow who can fly, and he hates me and Rose.'

Moss's tiny hand slips into mine. 'But *why*, Arthur?'

I can hardly tell her the truth: that Crowky hates us because we made him that way, because years ago, in Grandad's attic, we played a game where Rose pretended to be a scarecrow who loved trying to catch me and that this scarecrow then came to life in Roar. So instead I say, 'We don't know why. It's just the way he is.'

This isn't enough for Win. 'Crowky hates Arthur and Rose because he hates *everything* that's happy and good and fun! He made an army of scarecrows and tried to destroy Roar. He burned down the Lost Girls' camp. He kidnapped Arthur and Rose's grandad!' He goes on to tell the fairies all about The Box, and how Crowky wanted to use it to get to Home. 'That's how he ended up all alone in the sea. Arthur tried to save him, but he wouldn't leave the –'

I squeeze Win's arm to stop him from talking.

'Leave the what?' says Moss, her eyes darting from me to Win.

'Just . . . something that belonged to our grandad,' I say quickly. The fewer people who know about the T-shirt and what it can do the better.

'And what is *Home?*' asks Moss.

'It's where Arthur and Rose live when they're not in Roar,' replies Win. 'They do incredible magic there and it's full of amazing stuff like TVs and trampolines and rocky road and their grandad, Jay, who is the nicest person *ever.*'

'Look,' says Rose. 'All you really need to know is that Crowky is bad news. You've only ever seen him flying around, but he can use his hands to drain the life out of living things and turn them into scarecrows. He's done it to our grandad, Arthur and Win, and he'll do it to you too if he ever gets hold of you. Maybe that's why he was on your balcony, Moss.'

I thought the fairies would be horrified to discover who they've been sharing their island with, but instead they start laughing. 'And we thought he was a ghost!' says Owl.

'But Crowky is worse than a ghost,' I say. 'He can stuff you full of ice-cold straw just by pressing his hands down on your body!'

'I'd like to see him try to stuff Moss,' says Twig. 'She'd stuff him right back!'

All three of the fairies find this very funny. When they've stopped rolling around and giggling, Moss says. 'Don't worry about that stupid scarecrow, Arthur. I'll stay awake and if he comes back I'll get him. You three should go to sleep or you'll be too tired to sail away tomorrow.'

Suddenly Rose gasps. 'We forgot about Mitch! We need to go out to the *Alisha* and check that she's OK. We need to warn her about Crowky!'

'She'll be safe,' says Moss. 'She's got all those monkeys looking after her.'

Rose shakes her head. 'Even so, we need to tell her.'

Moss jumps to her feet. 'I'll go. I'll be quicker than you.'

I can see that Rose wants to go herself, but before I can say anything Moss dashes towards the staircase, calling over her shoulder, 'I'll be back in a minute!'

Rose is too fidgety to wait on the balcony. Even though it's still dark we go down to the beach. The first thing Rose does is check Mitch's hut. It's empty, just like we expected it to be, so we huddle together on the cool sand and stare out to sea.

The moon is bright, lighting a path towards the *Alisha*. Rose keeps her eyes fixed on this path, looking out for Moss's rowing boat. Win and I take it in turns to glance back into the jungle. We want to make sure Crowky doesn't creep up on us.

Unlike the three of us, Twig and Owl are perfectly relaxed and seem to be enjoying their middle-of-the-night trip to the beach. They keep jumping up to run around on the sand and they dart in and out of the sea, throwing luminous seaweed at each other. And they can't seem to stop talking even though I tell them to be quiet. They chatter on about how fast Moss can row, and then Owl reminisces about the time Twig beat Moss in a rowing competition and Moss was so angry she threw her boat at him.

'I turned it into a tree house before it could hit me!' Twig says, laughing.

'She's coming!' shouts Rose.

Moss's oars are a blur as they whip through the water. The rowing boat hits the beach so hard that it wedges into the sand. She jumps out and runs towards us. She's panting, tired out from her super-fast rowing, and for a moment she can't talk.

'How is Mitch?' says Rose. 'Is she OK?'

Moss looks up at Rose. 'She's gone!' she says. Her words make the beach seem darker and colder.

'Gone?' says Rose. 'What do you mean?'

'I looked all over the ship, in Mitch's cabin, down in the hold, everywhere, and it's *completely* empty. Mitch has disappeared and so have all the monkeys!'

CHAPTER 32

'She could have gone for a swim,' says Win.

We're all standing on the beach staring at the *Alisha*, trying to work out what's happened to Mitch.

'What about the orangutans?' says Rose. 'They hate getting wet!'

'Perhaps they've all gone for a night-time walk?' suggests Moss.

I'd love to believe this was true, but how could Mitch have got all the orangutans off the ship? And would she really have brought them to this island when she's so desperate to leave? I take out our map and stare at the tiny drawing of Crowky peering out of a window at the Crow's Nest. His eyes seem to lock on to mine.

'I know what's happened to them,' I say. 'Crowky's got them.'

Moss pats my shoulder. 'If he has, then we'll get them back.'

'And then what?' I say, because right now I feel like I can

173

never escape from Crowky.

'And then you'll go off in your big boat and leave him here,' says Moss. 'This island is like a prison. If you haven't got a boat like the *Alisha*, it's impossible to leave.'

A *prison* . . . That's just what we need for Crowky. 'But what about you?' I say. 'We can't leave you stuck here with him.'

The fairies look at each other and smile. 'Yes you can,' says Moss. 'He doesn't scare us.'

'*Really?*' I say.

She laughs. 'Yes, *really*! He can't stuff us, can he? If he tried, we'd chuck him in a tree! Anyway, it might be fun having someone else on the island. We can make him cakes.'

For the next few minutes, Rose, Win and I try to convince the fairies that living with Crowky really won't be fun and that he won't appreciate their baking, but they refuse to be bothered by him. In the end, Moss says, 'Forget about us, it's your mermaid we should be worrying about.'

'You're right,' says Rose. 'We need to start looking for her.'

A glimmer of sunlight has appeared on the horizon. Soon it will be light enough to go into the jungle so Moss sends Twig and Owl off to get food while she goes to check on her lighthouse. 'Crowky was on the balcony,' she says. 'I want to make sure he's not taken anything.'

'Do you want me to come with you?' I ask. I'd hate to go

back to that lighthouse on my own.

Moss bursts out laughing, 'No! What could you do?'

She's got a point. So Rose, Win and I stay where we are on the beach. While we wait, Win prowls up and down and Rose and I watch the sky grow lighter.

Knowing that Crowky is on this island, and that right now he could be lurking in the jungle, watching us, makes me jumpy. He must know we're here. He's probably been watching us ever since we arrived . . .

Suddenly I feel exhausted. Not from tiredness, but from running from Crowky. When we get off this island we might be able to leave Crowky behind, but he'll still have the T-shirt. That means I'm going to have to keep looking over my shoulder – in Roar, at Home, at school – waiting for the moment when he comes to get me. Because I know that he will . . . one day.

A sound makes me spin round.

'It's just the parrot,' says Rose.

I was so wrapped up in in my thoughts I hadn't noticed the green parrot perched on the roof of Mitch's hut. It starts to chatter away. Other birds call back to it from the jungle.

'I can't stop thinking about Crowky,' I say. 'He's on this island, Rose, and you know what he'll have with him.' I remember Crowky's fingers closing round Grandad's T-shirt as it floated in the sea. 'This is our chance to get it back!'

After a moment Rose says, 'Arthur, you're not going to like this, but you really need to forget about it. We need to find Mitch and the orangutans then get away from here. We haven't got time to do anything else.'

'But how long do you think it will take him to escape from this island?' I say. 'What he's got is a key, Rose, and it will let him into Home, and then what will he do? Grab hold of Grandad? Stuff him?' Then another, even worse, thought crosses my mind. 'Rose, he could open the bed! If he did that then *everything* would disappear, including Win and Mitch! There would be no more Roar!'

'Shhh!' says Rose angrily. She glances across at Win who right now is karate-chopping a wave. 'Crowky doesn't know about the bed, and neither does anyone else in Roar, and they can never find out. Arthur, can you imagine how they'd feel if they knew that the only thing holding their world together was a rusty old camp bed?'

Instantly I feel terrible. She's right. I should never have mentioned it.

'You're tired, Arthur,' she says in a softer voice, 'and worried. You'll feel better once we've found Mitch and the orangutans.'

There's a clatter of footsteps on the wooden hill then Twig and Owl run on to the beach. 'We've got chocolate buns and bananas!' shouts Twig.

'And coconut milk!' adds Owl.

The parrot gives an indignant squawk and flies away.

Perhaps Rose is right, I think, as I jump to my feet. *Perhaps it is time to forget about the T-shirt.*

CHAPTER 33

Moss arrives a few minutes later and suggests we split up. 'Once we get to the top of the wooden hill I'll go into the Bowl with Rose, and Twig can go with Arthur. We'll meet in the middle.'

'What about me and Owl?' says Win.

'You've got the most important job of all,' says Moss. 'Guarding the *Alisha*. You don't want Crowky sailing away on it, do you?'

We turn to look at the ship that's bobbing gently in the bay. I can't believe I didn't think about this myself. 'How can Owl stop him from doing that?' I ask.

'Show them, Owl,' says Moss.

Owl lifts his hands and starts to wriggle his fingers. Immediately the waves beyond the bay rise up. They crash over the rocks by the lighthouse. Their roar shatters the peace of the island.

'No one could sail through that!' says Moss triumphantly.

'What am I going to do?' asks Win, looking wistfully at

the jungle we're about to explore.

'You have to make sure Crowky doesn't sneak up on Owl and stop him from making the storm,' says Moss.

Win frowns, not entirely convinced that this is the 'most important job of all', but he accepts his fate, pulls out his wand and drops into a crouching position. 'I won't take my eyes off this jungle,' he says. 'You're safe with me, Owl!'

'Then let's go,' says Rose impatiently, and we leave Owl and Win and walk up the wooden hill.

When we reach the top we're already hot and sweaty. We stand and look down into the Bowl. The jungle below us is thick and tangled, and it looks like the perfect place to hide. I really don't want to go in there, but I know we have to if we're going to find Mitch and the orangutans.

Moss and Twig start bickering about which way to go and suddenly I feel uncertain about leaving Rose. 'Shouldn't we stick together?' I say.

Rose shakes her head. 'Look how big it is, Arthur. Unless we split up it will take us hours to find Mitch. Plus this way we'll each have a fairy; they know the way and they're strong.'

I remember the moment when Twig marched out of the jungle holding a pile of logs in his arms; if we bump into Crowky, then I'll be pleased he's by my side. 'Fine,' I say. 'But we need to be careful. You know what Grandad always says: stick together.'

'I know,' she says, 'but this is an emergency. He'd understand.'

Moss climbs over the rocky edge of the Bowl and takes a path leading to the left. 'Come on, Rose!' she calls.

I give Rose what I hope is a brave smile, then I follow Twig as he starts walking along a path that leads in the opposite direction. Soon we reach the edge of the jungle. Trees, vines and tangled flowers loom in front of us. Twig bounces on his toes, keen to get going. 'Come on, Arthur!'

'OK,' I say, 'but, Twig, we've got to be quiet. I know Crowky isn't a ghost, but we still don't want him jumping out on us.'

'Got it!' he says, and he's so excited he has to clamp his hand over his mouth to stop himself from giggling. Then he grabs my wrist and pulls me into the jungle.

CHAPTER 34

We creep under towering trees, breathing in the hot, damp air. Only a few spots of sunlight manage to break through the canopy and these shine down on us like spotlights. We push our way through ferns, great waxy flowers and thick leaves. We don't shout out for Mitch – we can't let Crowky know that we're coming. Instead we listen carefully and keep our eyes peeled for any sign of orangutan fur, bright blue hair or yellow straw.

But it's hard to see or hear anything down here in the Bowl. Vines tangle round us and we're surrounded by the constant clicking of insects. Plus it's so hot that soon sweat is trickling down my forehead and stinging my eyes.

'Twig, are you sure we're going the right way?' I ask, slapping my hand down on a biting insect. I haven't got a clue where we are.

'If we keep going towards the big spiky tree and then go left, we'll get to the middle of the island and the twisty tree where we're meeting Moss,' he says.

Twisty tree . . . spiky tree . . . they all look the same to me, but Twig seems to know where he's going. He strides ahead of me, using his strong hands to pull down any branches or vines that get in our way.

'*Spiky tree*,' he mutters, when we reach a tree with sharp needles poking out of the bark. 'Now we need to have a rest.'

We're in a small clearing. There is more light here and butterflies dart around in the sunshine. I sink on to a boulder and realise how tired I am. I only slept for a couple of hours last night, and walking through this jungle is as exhausting as wading through mud. The heat presses down on me like a blanket and I wish that I had some water. I drank my coconut milk ages ago.

I'm about to ask Twig if he knows some fairy way to get water out of plants, when Rose comes bursting into the clearing.

'What are you doing here?' I say. 'Where's Moss?'

'I don't know,' she says. 'I lost her back at the river. You know how fast she runs. I think she forgot that my legs don't work like hers.'

'Hello!' says Twig, grinning at Rose.

She frowns back at him. 'Hello . . . How come you're so happy?'

'You're here!' he says, and with that he spins round and heads back into the jungle, calling, 'Come on. I know where we're going!'

'We'd better follow him,' says Rose, pulling me to my

feet. 'Trust me. It's no fun being in this jungle on your own.'

Rose stomps ahead of me, pushing through the thick leaves. 'Hurry up, Arthur!' she calls whenever I drop too far behind.

'Are you sure this is the right way?' I ask.

'Twig knows what he's doing,' she says, followed by: 'Sorry, Arthur. I'm worried about Mitch and this place gives me the creeps. I just want to find her and get out of here.' She stops to pull a spider's web off her face.

'Me too,' I say, lifting a spider off her shoulder and letting it drop to the ground.

We carry on walking. It's so damp that moisture drips from the leaves and trickles over our skin. A gap has opened up between us and Twig and we're only just managing to keep up.

'Rose,' I whisper, 'do you get the feeling something funny is going on?'

The further we've got from the wooden hill and the fairies' beautiful platforms and their glow bugs in jars and delicious cakes, the more uneasy I've felt. The Bowl feels so different to the wooden hill: it's wild and full of shadows and frightening sounds. And now one of our guides has disappeared and the other one seems to be leading us deeper and deeper into the jungle.

'Perhaps . . .' she says. 'Why?'

'Well, Twig's been acting a bit strange. I know the fairies are always excited, but he seems to be loving this. He keeps hopping up and down and giggling. And Moss left you all on your own –'

'That could have been a mistake,' she says quickly, still trying to defend her beloved fairies.

'Maybe,' I say, 'but remember how Mitch said she could smell magic? Well, right now this jungle smells like a very old library *and* I can smell marzipan. The smell has been getting stronger ever since we bumped into you and Twig led us further into the jungle.'

She sniffs the air. 'I think you might be right . . .'

'I *am* right,' I say, and then I realise something. 'Oh no . . .'

Rose looks at me. 'What is it, Arthur?'

'The only person who searched the *Alisha* was Moss. What if Mitch never left the ship? She could be locked up below deck with the orangutans for all we know!'

'But why would Moss do that?'

'I don't know, but I think we should get out of this jungle and check the *Alisha* for ourselves!'

I'm about to turn round when Rose grabs my arm. 'Arthur, did you hear that?'

Up ahead Twig has stopped walking and is peering between two trees.

There is the sound of running water – we must be near the river that winds through the middle of the Bowl – and I can hear something else too.

'What *is* that?' I whisper.

'Wings!' she says, pulling me forward.

We creep towards Twig. I can hear the sound clearly now: a swish-swish of wings beating the air. They sound big and powerful. They sound familiar . . . Rose puts a finger to her lips. Keeping as quiet as possible, we wriggle closer to Twig.

'Look!' he whispers, eyes wide, then he pulls back a branch.

Crowky is standing in the middle of a clearing. His straw hair is standing on end and his wings are beating the air. Slowly he turns to face us.

CHAPTER 35

The sight of Crowky's inky-black button eyes makes my chest squeeze tight. My instinct is to run, but I stay exactly where I am because Crowky is staring into the jungle. Hardly daring to breathe I watch as his eyes move from left to right. His hair is scruffier than ever, wisps of straw stick up in all directions, and his sack face is deathly pale. His eyes settle on the spot where we are hiding.

Rose's hand finds mine and she squeezes it. *Keep quiet*, she's saying. She's usually calmer than me, and right now she's keeping as still as a statue and staring right back at Crowky.

He takes a step forward and his coat falls open. He's wearing his old grey shirt and there's no sign of Grandad's 'NO PROB-LLAMA!' T-shirt. Wildly I wonder if he left it in the sea. Perhaps all my worrying has been for nothing . . .

He bends down, picks up some sort of tool, then turns back to whatever it was he was doing. And that's when I see the dragon.

It's not a living, breathing dragon like Vlad or Pickle. It's a huge model

lying slumped on the ground with a tree-trunk body and wings made of burnt branches and sacking. Stitched into the wings are hundreds of feathers. Crowky walks round his creation, his own wings still beating fast, and a smile spreads across his face. He's happy, excited by what he's made. He turns to the river that runs alongside the clearing, dips a metal tool into the water then dries it on a strip of leather. Then he goes to the dragon's head, kneels and starts to scrape away at the lump of wood, carving the snout. No, it's not a snout, it's a curving beak.

Rose leans closer to me and whispers, 'He's made a crow-dragon!'

I nod because it doesn't feel safe to talk, then we carry on watching as Crowky takes a rag out of his pocket, opens the crow-dragon's mouth and starts to polish a row of sharp white teeth. What are they made of? Wood? Bone? From this distance it's hard to tell. Crowky spots something he's not happy about. He wobbles one of the teeth until it falls into his hand. Scowling, he jumps to his feet, then strides straight towards us.

Rose's hand tightens on mine and I hold my breath as Crowky crashes past us into the jungle. He's so close that if I reached out I could touch the edges of his flapping coat. Amazingly he doesn't see us. The rushing of the river must cover any sounds we're making and he's obviously got his mind on the broken tooth.

We stay where we are, listening as Crowky stomps deeper

into the jungle. We wait until at least a minute has passed, and then Rose grips my hand even tighter and says, 'This is our chance, Arthur!'

Before she can move, I blurt out, 'Rose, I think we should look for the T-shirt as well.'

'*The T-shirt*,' she repeats, then she smiles. 'Yes, we should, definitely! Come on!'

I'm surprised – last night she told me to forget all about it – but I guess this opportunity is too good to pass up.

Rose shoots out of the safety of the jungle and into the clearing. She moves so fast that she's reached the crow-dragon before I've even taken a step.

'Wait for me!' I hiss, running forward.

Twig stays in the forest while we search the clearing for any sign of Mitch, the orangutans or the T-shirt, but all we find are discarded tools and bits of crow-dragon.

'There's nothing here,' I say.

'We should check that cave.' Rose points towards a dark opening in the rock. It's covered in vines and so well hidden I'm amazed she even spotted it.

'I don't know,' I say, glancing over my shoulder. 'What if he comes back?'

Rose sighs with frustration. 'Arthur, we *have* to check that cave. Mitch could be in there and so could the T-shirt. Twig will keep a lookout.' Then she grabs my wrist and drags me forward. We pause at the entrance.

'We need to be as quick as possible,' she says. 'I'll look

for Mitch. You look for the T-shirt, got it?'

I nod, then she ducks into the cave and I follow.

We step into a gloomy chamber. It takes a second for my eyes to adjust, but then I see that the cave is large and stretches a long way back. There's a pile of ferns in one corner – Crowky's nest I'm guessing – and various tools, bits of fabric and drawings are scattered across the floor and arranged on stone shelves. Crowky is messy, but one thing is clear: Mitch isn't here.

'It doesn't matter,' says Rose, hiding her disappointment. 'We can still look for the T-shirt.'

Rose is right: if it's here we need to find it. I push aside rags and old bits of sacking, but I can't see the yellow 'NO PROB-LLAMA!' T-shirt anywhere.

'It's not here,' I say.

'Keep looking,' says Rose. 'Check the back of the cave. There's stuff there.'

'How do you know?' I say, but then I see a flash of yellow in the shadows at the back of the cave and realise that Rose is right; there's something there! I run forward and find a carved dragon's head sitting alone on a stone shelf. A piece of yellow fabric is stuffed inside. I shove my hand into the gaping mouth and pull out a T-shirt. The words 'NO PROB-LLAMA!' jump out at me.

'I've got it, Rose!' I shout, but she doesn't reply.

Instead a familiar scratchy voice snarls, 'NO!'

I spin round just as Crowky bursts into the cave.

Rose steps out of a dark corner and yells, 'Throw it to me, Arthur!'

'Don't!' cries Crowky, leaping towards me, but already my arm is pulling back and before he can take another step I hurl the T-shirt towards Rose.

It's a perfect throw. *Take that Mr McGill*, I think as it soars past Crowky's sack face and into Rose's waiting hands.

She grabs it and dashes out of the cave yelling, 'Go, Twig, GO!'

Crowky spins round and races after her and so do I, but after a few steps he lets out a cry of rage. Vines are shooting across the entrance of the cave, tangling round each other and growing faster and faster. In a few seconds my exit will be blocked! Crowky tries to pull the vines apart, but they keep on growing.

'Rose! Help!' I shout, pushing my arm through a gap in the leaves and reaching out to her. 'Please, Rose. Do something!'

But my words just make her step back and giggle. What's wrong with her? She doesn't seem to care that I'm trapped in here with Crowky! And that's when I see what Twig is doing: his arms are outstretched and his fingers are wriggling in the air. More vines burst across the opening, growing so fast that, before I know it, my arm is being crushed. Twig notices this and his hands fall to his side.

'Don't stop!' yells Rose, shoving him. 'Keep going!'

'But . . . I'm hurting him.'

'I DON'T CARE!' she screams, flinging his hands back up in the air. The vines start to grow again. Green shoots twist up my arm, moving towards my face. I jump back, yanking my arm free.

And that's when Crowky turns to look at me, his face filled with rage, and he hisses, 'Arthur Trout . . . *what have you done?*'

CHAPTER 36

Crowky's arm swings towards me and his fingers dig into my neck. '*Drain!*' he growls and instantly an icy cold slams into me. I try to prise his fingers away, but the chill spreads down my hands and arms and into my body. Panic races through me even faster than the cold: Crowky has stuffed me before and I know what's coming next. I take a deep breath and try to prepare myself for the moment when the prickly cold reaches my heart . . . but it doesn't happen.

Instead Crowky shoves me away, turns and stares out of the cave. I stumble forward, rubbing my neck. He's watching Rose. Something is happening to her . . . Her hands are pressed into her face and her whole body is shimmering. It's like I'm looking at her through rippling waves of heat.

'Rose!' I shout. 'Are you OK?'

She doesn't reply, she just stands there, her face hidden in her hands as the shimmering becomes more powerful. Now everything around Rose is trembling too – the leaves on the trees, the long grass, the feathers on the crow-dragon. She drops into a crouch and then, like a horrible magic trick, she starts to change in front of my eyes. Her long curly hair disappears, her arms become thin and her leopard-print onesie fades to green.

'Rose!' I pull at the vines. 'What's happening?!'

The shimmering disappears and the clearing returns to normal. A monkey calls out somewhere in the jungle and the sun shines down. Slowly Rose lowers her hands. Her brown eyes have gone and green eyes stare back at me. They're the colour of sea glass.

I'm looking at Moss.

I'm too shocked to speak. I look around the clearing and the edge of the jungle for Rose. Twig is there, standing to one side and smiling nervously, but Rose has vanished.

'Where's my sister?' I shout at Moss. 'What have you done with her?'

My confusion delights her and she laughs and claps her hands. 'She's stuck up a *tree*! You didn't know it was me, did you, Arthur? I totally tricked you! I left your sister on a platform at the top of a very tall tree and it was *sooo* easy. I told her we needed to go up there to find out where we were, then I bit her, climbed down the ladder and took it away!'

I shake my head. 'What are you talking about? Rose was here a second ago. I was talking to her!'

Next to me Crowky snarls with frustration. 'You were talking to *her*, you idiot, *Moss*! All fairies have a magical power, and this one, Moss, has the greatest power of all: she can steal the bodies of living creatures!'

'And I did it to *Rose*,' Moss cries. 'I stole her skin and you didn't even know!'

'Stop it, Moss,' says Twig. 'We're not supposed to talk about it, remember?'

She ignores him and carries on. 'Usually I only steal the skin of animals and birds, but I just grabbed hold of her, bit her and, whoosh –' she throws her arms up in the air – 'I became Rose!'

I stare at her in horror. 'You *bit* my sister? You're like a vampire!'

She scowls angrily. 'I'm not a *monster*, Arthur. I don't drink blood. I just did a teeny-weeny bite, sort of breathed in and borrowed Rose for a bit. I do it all the time. I'm really good at it. Remember that crab in Mitch's hut? That was me, and I was that sloth watching you when you were stuffing your face with cake!'

I think back to the hairy sloth that Rose fed from her hand, remembering how it stared at us so intently. 'But is Rose OK?' I ask.

Moss shrugs like she couldn't care less. 'Don't know. Probably. If she hasn't rolled off the platform, she'll wake up soon wondering why she's stuck up a tree.'

I notice that as Moss has been talking she's been glancing at the T-shirt that's clutched in her hands. Quickly she pulls it over her head. It's huge on her, like a tatty old dress.

She looks at me slyly. 'You really wanted this T-shirt, didn't you, Arthur?'

I think back over everything I said to Moss when I thought she was Rose. I'm sure I didn't mention what the T-shirt did, that it would let her into Home, but she looks very pleased to have it. 'I wanted it because it's my grandad's,' I say.

'No, it's not, it's MINE!' hisses Crowky.

Moss grins. 'Well, I've got it now and I'm taking it far away from here!'

Suddenly Crowky pounds on the vines. 'You were never going to take me with you, were you?'

'Maybe . . . to fly this thing.' She gives the crow-dragon's tail a kick. 'But now I've got the *Alisha* I don't need you or your rubbish Crowgon.'

Panic rises inside me. She's planning to take the *Alisha* and leave us here!

'I don't understand,' I say. 'If you wanted to leave, we could have sailed away together. We asked you to come with us, but you said that you loved it here!'

Moss laughs and steps closer to the vines. 'I LIED. I lie all the time. I *hate* this island and I have never, ever forgotten who trapped me here!'

I feel sick and for a moment I wonder if my legs might collapse beneath me.

Her smile vanishes and an ugly scowl takes its place. 'Those few words you shouted were the most powerful magic

I've ever encountered. I liked it in Roar. We were having *fun*, then I gave you one tiny little bite and you yelled, '*Send them to The End!*' and the next thing we knew we were here. Five words were all it took to steal my freedom. Well, guess what, Arthur? You shouldn't have sent us away because fairies are vengeful.' She grins, showing her teeth, and I'm almost pleased a tangle of vines separates us.

'What are you going to do?' I say.

'I'm going to steal something from you, Arthur. Something you love.' At this point she pulls a folded piece of paper out of her pocket and opens it. It's our map of

Roar. She must have taken it from Rose. 'The question is
. . . what's it going to be?' Just then a small yellow bird flies
down into the clearing. Without taking her eyes off the map
Moss's hand shoots up and grabs hold of the bird. Its wings
flutter in her fist. 'It's quicker to fly,' she says, then she opens
her mouth and bites the bird's neck with her pointed teeth.

I watch in horror as the bird struggles for a moment
before falling still. Moss drops the bird on the ground, then
covers her face with her hands, just like she did before. The
shimmering starts again. Moss and the bird both look as if
heat is rising around them. Then they start to fade. They
look like ghosts of themselves and just when I think they're
going to vanish completely there is a flash of light and there
are two birds in the clearing. One is still lying on the ground,
but the other, Moss, is flying in swooping circles.

The bird opens its beak, sings a triumphant song, then
flies away along the river.

'Moss!' shouts Twig. 'Wait!' He's about to run after her
when he pauses and looks back at me. 'Sorry about trapping
you and everything, Arthur.'

'Twig, you can't go,' I say. 'You've got to help me get out
of here!'

'No way,' he says, backing away. 'Moss would *kill* me if I
did that!' Then he turns and runs into the jungle.

The bird that Moss bit is lying on the ground. Its wings
are spread out and its tiny chest is rising and falling. Is this

what happened to Rose? When I was walking through the jungle thinking she was by my side, was she actually lying fast asleep like this bird?

For one blissful moment I'm relieved. Moss is gone and the bird doesn't look like it's hurt, which means Rose should be OK too, but then I realise how bad our situation is. Moss is about to take the *Alisha* and sail away to Roar. And she said she was going to steal something from me, but what? I remember her hungry look as she gazed at the map. Whatever she's planning to do, I've got to get out of here! Desperately I pull at the vines.

'It's no use.' The whispered words come from just behind me and I turn to see that Crowky has crept up on me. He sucks in his breath, narrows his eyes, then hisses, 'I'm going to get you, Arthur Trout!'

CHAPTER 37

I try to run, but I'm trapped. Crowky grabs hold of my shoulders.

'Do you know how long I've been stuck on this island with that fairy and her rages?' He pushes his face close to mine. '*Months* . . . You left me in that freezing sea. I couldn't fly, but I drifted with the currents. Sun burned the straw that was keeping me afloat. Fish nibbled my face, but I held tight to the T-shirt and eventually I washed up here and Moss pulled me out of the sea. She would have thrown me straight back in if she hadn't found out that we have something in common.' He shakes me hard. 'We both hate *you*, Arthur Trout!'

He digs his fingers into my skin and the cold bites into me so fast that I don't have time to breathe. 'Please . . . don't stuff me,' I whisper.

He shakes me hard. 'Give me one reason why I shouldn't!'

I swallow. My throat feels like straw. 'Because I've got to get out of here. I've got to help the others.'

He laughs and his wings spring out, brushing the cave walls. 'Wrong answer! Try again.'

My mind seems to be slowing down, but I desperately try to think of the right thing to say. 'Because we have to stop Moss from taking the *Alisha*, and two of us trying will be better than one!'

His hands squeeze tighter. The cold creeps into the middle of my body. It wraps round my heart and seeps into my lungs. I can hardly breathe. But then, without warning, Crowky shoves me to the ground and starts to prowl around the room.

I lie on the stone floor. My body feels like it's crammed full of freezing, scratchy straw and each breath is a struggle. If Rose or Win were here, they could take away the cold just by putting their hands on me. But I'm all alone with Crowky, so I lie where I am and wait for the feeling to go away.

Crowky slumps against the wall of the cave and watches me. He hardly blinks as I start to move my arms and legs and stretch out my fingers. He keeps his eyes glued on me as I stagger to my feet, grab a blanket off the floor and wrap it round my shoulders.

I go to the vines and try to pull them apart. I use every bit of strength I have, but they won't budge. They may be green and have shoots and leaves springing out of them but they might as well be made of steel. I pull at them until I have blisters on my fingers. I find a piece of wood on the floor and try to prise them apart. Nothing works. I only give up when out in the clearing the yellow bird flutters its wings.

It struggles to its feet, looks around, then flies into the air and disappears over the trees.

'Moss is back in her own body.' Crowky's scratchy voice makes me jump. 'She can only steal someone's skin for so long before their owner wakes up and claims it back.'

I think about what this means. Moss has easily had enough time to fly back to the wooden hill. She'll be on the boat by now, preparing to sail away!

Perhaps Crowky realises this too because something makes him leap into action. With a snarl he starts pulling at the vines. He's much stronger than me, but even so he can't make the gaps any bigger. He hunts around his cave and finds a tool and uses this to hack at the twisted shoots. Nothing works, but he doesn't give up.

It's only when the sun starts to sink below the trees that he goes to the far side of the cave and drops to the ground. His wings tremble as he glares at me. We're as far away as we can possibly get from each other, but his rage still reaches me. His hands are balled into fists. Deep lines mark his sack face and his button eyes glitter in the gloom, and they never leave my face.

CHAPTER 38

Beyond the vines, birds chirp in the jungle, the river bubbles and shadows grow longer. The Crowgon lies in the clearing like a great dog guarding the entrance to the cave.

Moss must have set sail by now, presumably with Owl and Twig as her crew. I think about what she said – *I'm going to steal something from you* – and I try to work out what she's planning to do. Panic rises in me again. Last night we told her so much about Roar – the Lost Girls, the dragons, the unicorns, Prosecco . . . Is she going to hurt one of them? Then I remember the T-shirt that I threw to her and my chest squeezes tight. Does she know that the T-shirt can let her into Home?

To take my mind off Crowky's staring eyes and the thought of Moss sailing away with the T-shirt, I look through the vines and study the Crowgon.

It's bathed in a soft golden light. Just like a real dragon, Crowky has given it spikes that go down its back and each of these spikes is carved out of dark wood. The feathers on the Crowgon's outstretched wings tremble in the breeze. There must be hundreds of them and I wonder how long it took Crowky to attach them all.

'Did Moss help you make it?' I say, breaking the silence.

'*Moss?*' he spits. 'I didn't let her touch a single feather. The Crowgon is all mine.' He can't resist moving to the entrance of the cave to gaze at his creation. It's getting dark now and the Crowgon's eyes glow bright red, lighting up the clearing.

'How did you make its eyes?' I ask.

For a moment he doesn't reply then he mutters, 'Coal.'

'But they look like they're burning.'

He turns to glower at me. 'I can make things come alive, Arthur Trout.' In the darkness he wriggles his stick fingers. They scrape against each other. '*These* can make things come alive.'

We fall back into silence. I think about Crowky's army of scarecrows and his spy crows. We've often wondered how he made them move and fly. Now I know.

The light fades. The Crowgon's eyes glow even brighter.

'Why haven't you flown away on it?' I ask.

Crowky scowls. 'Even with my hands and the fairies' magic I can't make it stay in the air. I thought Owl's storms would help, but it crashed to the ground and took me weeks to repair. Owl makes storms. Did you know that?'

I nod. 'And he stops them. He stopped the storm that brought our ship here.'

Crowky laughs bitterly. 'You idiot. He *made* that storm. Well, Moss told him to do it.'

I remember Owl's outstretched hands and the fierce look of concentration on his face. I thought he was pushing the wind away, but now I realise that he was using it to pull us closer. Mitch was right. The fairies tricked us from the very beginning.

Crowky carries on. 'It infuriates Moss that Owl can make storms but can't stop them. This island is surrounded by currents and waves too powerful for their little wooden boats. They've tried to escape, but their boats get smashed against the rocks. Moss said flying was the only way to get off this island. My wings have healed, but I can't fly far so I made the Crowgon.' His voice swells with pride. 'Moss brought what I needed – tools, wood, coal, coral, metal – and I did the rest. Her tail is made of ebony and her teeth are polished stone. She can breathe fire!' He stops talking and his hands tighten on the vines. 'I can make her stand, I can make her heart beat and I can make her wings move . . .'

'But you can't make her fly,' I say.

He stares at the Crowgon and says bitterly, 'Not yet . . .'

'How do your hands bring things to life?'

'To drain the life out of someone I press my fingers down and I feel *hate*.' His fingers twitch; he looks like he's tempted to demonstrate this right now. 'But when I bring something to life, that's different. I have to feel the opposite of hate. It's hard, but I managed it when I made my scarecrow army

206

and crows.' He looks at his dragon again. 'I came so close with the Crowgon.'

He obviously feels like he's said too much because he stomps to the back of the cave and throws himself down on his nest.

And so begins the strangest night of my life.

CHAPTER 39

For a long time Crowky stares at me and I try to ignore him. To begin with I turn my back on him and look at the clearing. I'm hoping to see Rose or Win. I even try calling their names, but the only response I get is a snigger from Crowky.

When it's dark in the clearing except for the Crowgon's glowing eyes, Crowky lights a torch. He does this carefully, and as he moves, his wings rustle and the straw in his body crackles. I shiver and his eyes shoot across to me. He doesn't miss a thing.

In the flickering light of the torch I can't resist glancing at him and I start to see things I've never noticed before. His black jeans are patched with a faded red fabric and his twig fingers are very long. He can't keep them still. He drums them on the ground, scratches the straw on his head and pulls at a loose thread that's hanging from his face.

When my legs become stiff from sitting hunched up I decide to stretch them. At first I walk up and down, sticking to the entrance, but after I've done this for a while, and Crowky hasn't pounced on me, I become bolder. I move deeper into the cave and look at the things he's put on the shelves hollowed out of the rock. I even dare to pick up a thin piece of bark that's weighed down by a stone.

Drawn on it is a picture showing two stick figures. One is clearly Crowky – I can tell by the wings. The other looks like a fairy because it's smiling and has pointed teeth. At first I think it's Moss but then I see a bird sitting on her shoulder and a snail on the palm of her hand.

I look at Crowky. 'Is this Pebble?'

'Put that down,' he hisses. Then, when the picture is back under its stone, he carries on talking. 'At first Moss didn't tell the other fairies I was on the island. She keeps secrets from everyone. She said that I was a ghost and that was enough to keep Owl and Twig away, but Pebble is braver than them. She would sneak away from Moss and visit me. She brought me water and fish. She was –' he pauses here as he searches for the right word – 'kind. But one day Moss found her here and flew into one of her rages. Do you know what she did? She tied Pebble to a boat then pushed the boat out into the wildest part of the sea!'

'Pebble is safe,' I say quickly. 'Her boat made it to another island.'

He stares at me. 'You've seen her?'

I nod. 'She didn't talk, but she seemed happy.'

'She used to talk. She wouldn't shut up!' Just when

I think Crowky is about to smile, he scowls. Then he says, 'We played this,' and he jabs at something next to him.

I'm forced to move closer so I can see what he's talking about.

On the ground is a square board marked with a grid. Little pieces are lined up opposite each other.

'It's chess!' I say. I've never seen a chess board in Roar, but it makes sense that there would be one because I've always loved playing it. It was Grandad who taught me to play and he's the only person I have never been able to beat.

'It's not *chess*,' says Crowky with heavy scorn. 'It's called I'm Coming to Get You.'

Which is exactly what Grandad whispers under his breath before he plays a killer move.

Crowky picks up the king and holds the carved figure between his long fingers. 'This is the boy,' he says, 'and it's the worst piece because it can only move one space at a time.' He puts it down and picks up the queen, only on Crowky's board it's a bird with outstretched wings. 'This is the crow and it can fly anywhere it likes, but only in a straight line.' He puts the crow carefully back in its place and then continues to tell me the names of all the I'm Coming to Get You pieces – unicorns, Lost Girls, ninja wizards and merwitches. This takes quite a long time as he can't resist telling me about his 'most devastating moves'. 'Once I beat Pebble before she'd had time to eat an apple.' A smile plays at the corner of his mouth. 'I really got her that time!'

My legs are starting to ache so, without thinking, I sit down opposite him.

'And that's how you play,' he says, putting the tiny merwitch (the knight) back in its place. There's a pause when neither of us talk. I'm just wondering if I need to stand up and get back in my corner when he mutters, 'I'm going first,' and moves a unicorn forward one space.

I stare from the board to Crowky. Am I about to play a game of chess with my arch-enemy? Suddenly his hand whips forward and he grabs the front of my T-shirt, pulling me closer. 'It's your go!' he hisses into my face before shoving me away again.

So I pick up a unicorn and with shaking hands I make my move.

CHAPTER 40

I wake up to the sound of my name being called again and again, 'Arthur! ARTHUR!'

Peering through the leaves, I see Rose and Win burst into the clearing. 'Over here!' I shout, tugging at the vines. To my surprise they fall away in my hands. Rose and Win run over and start pulling them away from the other side.

'He's here!' Win shouts over his shoulder. 'We've found him!'

There's a splash and Mitch heaves herself out of river. She looks furious. 'Those flipping fairies stole my boat, Arthur!'

'I know,' I say, glancing towards the back of the cave. Crowky is awake and standing in the shadows. He looks dangerous again. His eyes are narrowed and he's hunched forward as if he's ready to attack.

I'm not sure what I can do to calm him down so I try a smile. I get a growl in return.

Last night Crowky won both games of I'm Coming to Get You. I was determined to let him win the first game, but after he easily took me to checkmate, or 'got you' in his version, I couldn't resist trying to beat him the second time round. He won easily. After cackling triumphantly, and for a long time, he suddenly turned his back on me and pulled his wings over his face. Clearly it was bedtime.

'I saved us, Arthur!' says Win as light floods into the cave. 'Owl said I should swim out to a rock where I'd have a better view of Crowky then he made this crazy storm appear out of nowhere and I was stuck. Luckily he forgot to take my wand so all night, except for the bit when I was asleep, I did spells to escape. I tried doing *ant flongle* at dawn and that's what finally broke Owl's magic. The storm faded before my very eyes!'

'Yeah, maybe it was *ant flongle*,' says Mitch sarcastically, 'or maybe those fairies got so far away in *my* boat that their magic stopped working.'

Win's eyes widen. '*Ant flongle* is a mighty spell, Mitch. Its powers can be felt far and wide. Look, the magic even reached Arthur and untangled these vines!'

Mitch shakes her head as Rose pulls down the last twisty vine blocking my exit. I step out into dazzling sunshine.

'Look, Arthur.' Rose shows me a circle of bite marks on her wrist. 'Moss *bit* me, and – with Crowky's help – she locked Mitch inside her lighthouse. We got her seriously wrong.'

'I know,' I say, and quickly I tell them what happened after we split up yesterday. As I'm talking I'm aware that

Crowky is still standing behind me in the cave, and that at some point I need to tell the others he's there. Only what will I say? 'Oh, one other thing, I had a sleepover with Crowky last night. We played chess and he only tried to stuff me twice!'

'I can't believe Moss was pretending to be me,' says Rose, shuddering at the thought.

'She wasn't *pretending* to be you,' I say, 'she *was* you. Everything was the same: your hair, your clothes, even the way she said "Arthur" in your narky voice.'

Rose shakes her head in amazement. 'So *that's* her secret power. I knew it had something to do with biting . . .'

Mitch slams her tail down in the river. 'I told you that she ponged of magic!'

'What *is* this thing?' says Win. He's crouched in front of the Crowgon and is staring into its eyes. He reaches out a hand to stroke its wooden snout. 'Did Twig make it with his growing trick?'

'No he did not!' Crowky steps out of the cave. His hands are balled into fists and his wings are bristling.

Win pulls out his wand and Rose yells, 'Get back, Arthur!'

'No,' I say, holding up my hands. 'Please . . . put your wand away, Win.'

'But it's *Crowky*!' says Win, as if this explains everything.

I have to prove to them that we can trust him, at least until we get off this island. So I stand as close as I dare to Crowky and I say, 'I know, and we need his help.'

Rose shakes her head. 'Arthur, all he has ever tried to do is hurt us. Why would he help us?'

'Because he wants to get off this island just as much as we do.' Quickly I tell them about Moss's threat to steal something from me. 'It could be anything in Roar,' I say, 'the Lost Girls, the unicorns, Prosecco. She's got the map and she's heading there right now . . . And there's something else. She's got the T-shirt.'

Rose's eyes widen. 'But *how?*'

'I gave it to her,' I'm forced to admit. 'I thought she was you, Rose! But I'm sure she doesn't know what it can do. We need to get off this island and get back to Roar and stop her before she can hurt anyone.'

Suddenly Rose gasps and says, '*The dragons!*'

'Yes!' I say. 'They can help us. Moss might be crazily strong, but she's nothing compared to Bad Dragon.'

'That's not what I mean,' says Rose. 'What if Moss *becomes* Bad Dragon? Last night she was fascinated by them, remember?'

Silence falls over the clearing. None of us talk as we imagine the damage Moss could do if she became Bad Dragon . . . She could destroy everything in Roar!

It's Crowky who breaks the silence. 'My Crow's Nest is made of wood. She could burn it to the ground.'

'Forget about the Crow's Nest,' snaps Rose. 'What about the Lost Girls? They could be inside, but you don't care about them, do you? You've burned their home down once before. I bet you'd love to see it happen again!'

Fury twists Crowky's face. With just two steps he reaches Rose and grabs the front of her onesie, pulling her face close to his. 'I *was* thinking about them!' he snarls.

They stare at each other and I have the feeling that if Rose doesn't say the right thing, very quickly, then we are never getting off this island.

'Sorry,' she mutters. 'I'm worried. That's all.'

Crowky pushes her away and goes to stand by his Crowgon.

'Listen,' I say. 'We need to work together. We need to *help* each other.'

'How exactly can Crowky help us, Arthur?' says Mitch. 'Has he got a massive boat stashed away somewhere?'

'I've got something better than a boat,' Crowky snarls. 'I've got this!'

We stare at Crowky's creation. It's lying flopped on the ground like a puppet with its strings cut.

'That thing flies?' says Rose, her voice filled with doubt.

'*Imaginary!*' whispers Win.

'Almost,' says Crowky. 'I can bring it to life.'

'He needs help getting it in the air,' I say. 'Mitch, couldn't you make a storm or a wind that would help it fly?'

Mitch thinks for a moment. 'Possibly,' she says, looking at the bottles hanging round her neck. 'There's tons of stuff I could use in Moss's lighthouse, and this island is full of ingredients.'

'It's got to be worth a try,' I say, 'but we need to be quick.'

Win tugs at my sleeve. 'Remember I'm magic too, Arthur. I can help.'

Crowky does a bark of laughter at exactly the same time as Mitch – and then they glare at each other.

'Of course you can,' I say to Win. 'Together the three of you will make the Crowgon fly.'

CHAPTER 41

Mitch sends Rose and Win into the jungle to look for ingredients and then swims off down the river. She's going back to Moss's lighthouse to 'steal stuff'.

I'm left with Crowky. Although the others don't say it, I get the impression I'm being left to guard him, or, rather, make sure he doesn't somehow fly away on the Crowgon, our only way of getting off this island.

Crowky ignores me. He circles the Crowgon, arranging its limbs, tightening joints here and there, brushing away the odd loose feather. Then he sits cross-legged in front of it, his coat spread out behind him.

'Now I'm going to bring it to life,' he says. I'm not sure if this is a warning, or if he's showing off, but I decide that I'll be safer watching from the cave.

He stretches his hands out in front of him and wriggles his fingers. They click and clack as they move against each other. Then he places them on the forehead of his dragon and shuts his eyes. At first I don't think anything is happening. Then the very tip of the dragon's tail twitches. Crowky presses his hands down hard. Slowly, slowly the dragon's wings start to open. The tips stretch across the clearing, brushing the edge of the jungle and creeping towards my feet. Then Crowky lifts his hands and the Crowgon's head lifts too, as if it's glued to the tips of his fingers. Crowky stands and the huge wooden dragon lumbers to its feet.

It doesn't look like a puppet now. It looks alive. It looks dangerous. Its glowing eyes slide in my direction and narrow. Its leather eyelids blink.

The Crowgon might be coming to life, but Crowky seems to be getting weaker.

His face is even paler than usual and, as the Crowgon beats its wings, his own wings droop. His face is twisted with pain and effort, but he keeps pressing his fingers down and only stops when smoke starts to seep from the Crowgon's gaping mouth.

He staggers back, dropping to his knees and the Crowgon steps forward and sniffs his straw head.

And that's when Mitch comes back.

Cautiously she pulls herself out of the river and sits with her tail in the water. The Crowgon swings round and on creaking joints it staggers towards her. Her hand reaches for one of her bottles, but Crowky starts making the clicking noises that he uses to control his scarecrows and the Crowgon stops just short of Mitch.

It opens its mouth and breathes smoke over her. Mitch

stays exactly where she is, chin raised high, refusing to back away.

They stay like this, staring at each other as Crowky pushes past me and starts throwing things into a bag. In go the I'm Coming to Get You board and pieces, some tools and bits of wood and stone. Just then Rose and Win come running into the clearing. The Crowgon turns to look at them and they skid to a halt.

'Whoa!' says Win.

'Gobood gobirl,' says Rose, automatically using the language that she uses to control her dragons. But it doesn't work on the Crowgon. It huffs and puffs, swinging round and forcing me to jump away from the tail. Its mouth snaps open, but a couple of clicks from Crowky make it back away.

As Rose and Win share what they have found with Mitch, and she makes a potion on a slab of rock, I take one last look around the cave. That's when I notice that the picture of Pebble is gone.

'Come on, Arthur,' calls Rose. 'We've got to go!'

I find Mitch filling her bottles with the potion and Crowky whispering in the Crowgon's ear. Win, Rose and I stand awkwardly by the Crowgon, not sure who is in charge.

'So . . . shall we just climb on?' I say.

Mitch shudders as she hauls her tail out of the river. 'Sorry about this, tail,' she says. 'You're not going to like this.' Then she pulls herself across the ground towards us.

The Crowgon is big, but not big enough for five.

I suppose Crowky made it imagining he'd be carrying four small fairies as passengers. Win is the first person brave enough to scramble on to her back.

'It's comfy,' he says, shifting around and grabbing hold of a spike. 'Not as hot as the dragons and a bit smoother. Ow!' He winces. 'More splinters, though.'

Rose and Mitch climb up behind him, leaving me the space closest to the dragon's head. It looks like I'm next to Crowky then.

He gives the Crowgon one final stroke then jumps up and sits in front of me. Staring straight ahead he growls, 'Is the spell ready?'

Mitch uncorks the first bottle and shakes out the contents. I'm not sure if it's liquid or smoke, but it swirls like a miniature storm in the palm of her hand. 'I've made as much potion as I can,' she says, 'but I'm not sure how long it will last. Hopefully it won't run out when we're halfway over the Bottomless Ocean.' She chuckles at the thought, but I don't. We have to reach Roar before Moss. This has got to work.

'What even is that stuff?' asks Rose as the cloudy liquid rises into the air.

'I made a great big wind,' she replies, and Win sniggers. 'There's nothing funny about my wind, Win. In fact, it's so deadly it could knock you off this dragon.' This is too much for Win and he howls with laughter. Mitch ignores him and carries on. 'What I'm saying is that the moment

221

I let this spell go you're all going to have to hold on tight, at least until this thing is up in the air. Do you understand?'

Quickly we grab hold of the wooden spikes.

'Ready?' growls Crowky, and the Crowgon stretches out its wings.

'Ready,' says Mitch, and she tosses her swirling spell into the sky.

'Mitch has unleashed her deadly wind!' shouts Win, but he shuts up when a gale-force gust of air slams into us.

I'm almost thrown to the ground as it hits us, flattening the tops of the trees and making the Crowgon stagger to one side. The dragon starts to beat its wings and Crowky urges it on, but we don't lift up in the air. In fact, the wooden dragon looks like it's about to fall apart. Feathers swirl past my face and scales rattle. Its tail whips from side to side.

'Why's it not working?' I shout to Crowky.

'It needs more fire in its belly!'

I look back at the others. 'What can we do? Mitch, do you have a spell that can make fire?'

'*I* can make fire,' says Win, and before anyone can stop him, he's jumped off the Crowgon's back and run to stand in front of her. The sight of Win drives her wild. She leaps forward, gnashing her flinty jaws.

'What do you think you're doing?' snarls Crowky.

Win doesn't flinch. He pulls out his wand and yells, 'Mister Flambaygo!'

A ball of fire grows from the end of his wand. Sparks

burst from it as it gets bigger and bigger. 'Get that thing away from my dragon!' shouts Crowky, but Win ignores him and steps closer. The Crowgon roars. When its jaws are stretched wide open Win flicks his wand, sending the ball of flames into her gullet.

Immediately the Crowgon's wings start to pound up and down and she leaps forward. Fire glimmers from her joints and her back starts to heat up. I reach down and grab hold of Win's hand just as the dragon lifts up in the air. He scrambles behind me as we shoot higher and higher.

Behind me the others laugh and shout with joy. 'We did it!' screams Mitch. 'We actually did it!'

The Crowgon flies over the Bowl and then we're soaring over the wooden hill and out to sea. Crowky stares straight ahead, his hands resting protectively on the Crowgon's neck.

Her wings rise and fall. Smoke drifts from her carved nostrils. I lean forward. 'She's amazing!' I say.

'*I know,*' he replies with a snarl.

CHAPTER 42

The Crowgon is incredibly fast. Crowky has given her huge wings and Mitch's wind potion keeps her high in the air and racing forward. I cling to my wooden spike and peer over the dragon's wooden sides. First we're flying over mile upon mile of deserted sea, then we start to pass the islands we visited. It took us several days to cruise between them, but on the Crowgon we pass over them in a couple of hours.

Win chatters away, pointing out all the things he can see.

'I spy a baby hairy manatee!' he says, followed by, 'Wow! Is that a *yellow* penguin? Awesome!'

'It's a golden petrel,' snarls Crowky, unable to resist correcting him.

Soon Win gets bored of nature spotting and gets hungry instead. He's brought food with him and as we cover more and more miles, he shares it out, tossing apples, muffins and nuts up and down the Crowgon.

'Banana, Crowky?' he says, then, without waiting for a

reply, he lobs it towards him.

The banana hits Crowky on the shoulder then tumbles towards the sea. In a flash Crowky pushes past me and grabs Win's shoulders. '*Drain!*' he hisses. '*Drain!*'

'Burly husky,' Win whispers, flicking his wand. It turns into a sparkler, fizzing away and sending sparks spitting in all directions.

'*WIN!*' Mitch bellows after a spark scorches her tail. She uncorks a bottle and makes a puff of noxious yellow explode into his face. The wind she's been so carefully controlling fades for a moment and the Crowgon drops through the sky like a stone.

Now we're all screaming and shouting and sparks and smoke and nuts are flying everywhere.

'STOP IT!' shouts Rose.

And amazingly everyone does stop it. Crowky glares at Win then faces forward and Mitch goes back to sprinkling her wind spell around us.

Looking slightly guilty, Win puts away his wand and starts cracking nuts.

'Can we agree not to do any stuffing or unnecessary magic on the Crowgon?' I say.

'*No,*' says Mitch.

'Agreed!' says Win, reaching forward to offer Crowky his hand.

Crowky responds by grabbing hold of it and draining him for a second. He only stops when I pull them apart.

'Just . . . leave each other alone,' I say.

For the next half an hour all is peaceful, but then Win decides to while away the time by beatboxing. 'Listen to this, Arthur,' he says. 'Your grandad taught me this.' Then he starts saying 'boots and cats' again . . . and again . . . and again.

'Bootsandcatsandbootsandcatsandbootsandcatsand –'

Crowky spins round to glare at Win. His fingers twitch. 'Say that one more time and I'm going to throw you overboard to be eaten by sharks!'

'*Boots and cats*,' whispers Win, followed by, 'Sorry. That was it. I've finished . . . *Boots and cats*. Done.'

Crowky gives him a look that sends a chill down my spine.

'Seriously, Win,' I say. '*Shut up.*'

'I'm trying, Arthur,' he says, 'but it's really catchy!'

But somehow he manages it, and all is quiet until Mitch starts complaining about her itchy tail. 'It's the sun,' she says. 'It's drying it out. If I don't cool it down my scales will fall off . . . Arghhhh! So itchy!'

Luckily for Mitch we leave the heat of the Bends behind us as we fly closer to The End. Soon icebergs are floating past below us and when snow starts to fall Mitch sighs with relief. 'Bliss!' she cries, flipping her tail back and forth to catch as many snowflakes as possible.

It's not bliss for the rest of us. It's absolutely freezing, and even the heat rising from the Crowgon can't keep us warm. By the time we reach Barracuda Bay my toes and fingers are numb and my face feels like a block of ice. We fly over the village in seconds, glimpsing the rickety houses and the Bucket of Blood. 'Look,' I say, leaning towards Crowky. 'Your scarecrow army are down there, just where you left them.'

'Minus a very distinguished top hat!' says Win, tipping the brim of the hat he's been wearing all through our expedition.

Not for much longer, though . . .

'That doesn't belong to you!' snarls Crowky, and with a flick of his wrist he smacks the hat off Win's head and sends it spinning down to the ground.

Win watches it go with sad eyes, but he knows better than to complain. Instead he pulls his cloak a little tighter round him to make sure Crowky can't see his slashed scarecrow waistcoat.

It's when we're starting the most difficult part of our journey – our flight over the mountains at The End – that Win decides he needs a wee. He claims it's the sight of the gushing waterfall that does it. Whatever the reason, as the Crowgon rises higher and higher into increasingly cold air, he starts begging Crowky to stop for a toilet break, and his cry of, 'I need a wee!' becomes almost as annoying as 'boots and cats'.

'We're not stopping!' hisses Crowky. 'We have to get ahead of the *Alisha*!'

He's right, and Win must accept this because a few minutes later he announces, 'I'm fine! I think my wee has frozen!'

Rose, Mitch, Win and I huddle together as we pass over endless snowy peaks. Crowky curls closer to his Crowgon, snow settling on his shoulders and straw hair. When I reach forward to offer him one of our blankets, he pushes my hand away.

We're all relieved when we reach the sea again, particularly as Mitch has started to tell us she's running low on wind potion.

'I've got enough to get us to Roar,' she says, squinting at her bottle. 'Probably . . . If we're lucky.'

CHAPTER 43

Crowky guides the Crowgon over the Vampire – a frozen waterfall that Hati Skoll and her wolves chased us into – and towards the wall of mountains that separate The End from the rest of Roar. To pass through, we usually have to sail between a narrow gap in those mountains, but this time we simply soar over them.

We cross the Bottomless Ocean, the Crowgon's shadow floating over the waves, and we search for the *Alisha*. This is where we had hoped to find and overtake the ship, but all we can see is mile upon mile of white-tipped waves. I start to worry. We know that Owl can magic up storms. Could he have used this power to speed the ship along? Could they already be in Roar?

This thought is almost unbearable. My chest squeezes tight as I picture Moss opening our map, and deciding which of the many things I love that she's going to steal first . . . Then I imagine her creeping up on Bad Dragon and sinking her teeth into her.

Win leans forward. 'Arthur, are you all right?' I look down at my hands and realise they're shaking.

'Just cold,' I say, pulling my blanket closer round me.

Suddenly Crowky points into the distance. '*There!*'

Far ahead a dark shape is rising and falling with the waves. Win passes me the binoculars. Crowky is right. It's the *Alisha*!

We all take turns looking and then Mitch says, 'They're going fast. They'll reach Roar before sunset. We need to speed up!'

Crowky clicks an instruction, digging his knees into the Crowgon's side, but instead of shooting forward we turn to the left. I grab hold of a wooden spike to stop myself from sliding off its back. 'Crowky, what are you doing?' I yell. 'We need to overtake them, not fly in the other direction!'

Crowky turns and glowers at me. 'You really are stupid, aren't you? We don't want them to know we're here. We'll circle round them and land in Roar without Moss even knowing we've left the island. Then we'll hide those dragons and when Moss is least expecting it, we *strike!*' His hand slices through the air.

'Right,' I say. 'Good plan.' I'm starting to see that having a villain on our side has its advantages.

He urges the Crowgon to fly faster and it's not long before we see the grim shape of the Crow's Nest rising out of the sea.

As Crowky stares down at his castle, feathers start to

float past my face. At first I think they're coming from Crowky's wings, but then I see a clump break free from the Crowgon. We're slowing down too. Each thrust of the Crowgon's wings makes its body shudder and I can hear a strange rattle coming from somewhere inside it.

'What's wrong with the Crowgon?' I say.

'Nothing,' Crowky hisses. 'There's no wind!'

I turn round and see that Mitch is rifling through her bottles. 'It's fine,' she says. 'I know I've got one bottle left . . . It must be here somewhere!'

'Look!' shouts Rose. 'Roar!'

We've sailed through a cloud and suddenly land is ahead of us. I can see the cliffs and rocky mountains of the Bad Side, grey and menacing, and in the distance the Good Side. The Rainbow River twists through a flower-filled valley and beyond this the Tangled Forest rises over Roar, a great swaying canopy of green.

My heart lifts as I greedily take in the golden beaches and the deep indigo of the Bottomless Ocean. We're home!

Suddenly the Crowgon drops to one side. Win yelps and grabs hold of me and I cling to a spike. More feathers fly from its wings. 'Have you found that bottle, Mitch?' I shout.

'No. This will have to do!' I turn to see her dribble the last drops from an almost empty bottle into her hand. It's a tiny amount and it sits in her palm like a small puddle of silver. 'It won't get us far,' she admits, before tossing it up into the air.

The Crowgon surges forward, but it's still tilting to one side and something is grinding inside it. We drop lower in the sky and smoke begins to pour from the dragon's wooden scales. I cough and try to cover my eyes, then the spike I'm holding breaks off in my hands.

'Crowky!' I shout. 'It's falling apart. We need to land!'

He turns to glare at me through button eyes. 'What do you think I'm doing?'

Crowky urges the Crowgon to turn towards the beach. He nudges it with his knees and clicks instructions. I want to believe that we're safe and that Crowky can land this thing, but the reality is that we're sitting on a wooden crow-dragon that's hurtling down, and the only thing keeping it in the air are some home-made wings and a smidgen of magic.

We drop lower and lower in the sky until we're flying just over the sea. The beach is racing towards us . . .

'HOLD ON!' I yell and Win throws his arms round my waist.

We slam down in the sand. The jolt sends me up in the air then down again. I grab hold of something and I manage to hold on as the Crowgon skids sideways across the beach. The sand slows us down, but we're going too fast to stop. We crash over sand dunes then into a meadow. Sunflowers shoot past my face and I squeeze my eyes shut. There's another thud and I feel the Crowgon spin in a circle, then, finally, we come to a stop.

For a moment there is a buzzing in my ears, then I hear

birds singing and the hum of insects . . . and Win's hysterical laughter.

'We did it!' he cries. 'We beat Moss back to Roar!'

I open my eyes and see the beautiful sight of Roar spread out around me: tall golden grass sways in the meadow and the blue sea twinkles in the distance.

'Get off me,' hisses Crowky, and I realise that my hands are clamped tight round his waist.

'Sorry,' I mutter, letting go. I'm about to scramble off the Crowgon's back when it tilts forward.

'What's happening?' shouts Rose.

'A HOLE!' cries Win, and we plunge into darkness.

CHAPTER 44

A circle of curious faces peer down at us through a cloud of smoke and feathers. I see swinging plaits, muddy cheeks and ripped T-shirts. It's the Lost Girls. I don't think I've ever been so happy to see them.

'Arthur? Rose? Is that you?' shouts Stella.

'Yes!' I call back, pulling a wooden scale out of my knee. We're in a heap at the bottom of a deep hole surrounded by the smashed-up Crowgon.

'I'm trapped under Arthur!' comes a muffled voice, and I stand up to let Win escape.

'Hi, Rose!' calls Stella, spotting my sister buried under a pile of feathers. 'The girls were doing a bit of treasure hunting for Marmite when we saw you crash land. What's that thing you're sitting on?'

'A Crowgon,' I say.

Suddenly one of the Lost Girls starts jumping up and down and screaming. 'Crowky alert! CROWKY ALERT!

He's in the hole!'

Crowky drags himself out from underneath the Crowgon's heavy tail. His wings are crumpled and his head is turned sideways. With a quick twist, he gets it back into place.

'Get him, girls!' says Stella and a collection of wooden swords and sharp arrows are drawn and pointed at Crowky.

'No,' I say, scrambling to stand in front of him. 'You can't hurt him. He's helping us!'

Stella lowers her sword and raises one eyebrow. 'Arthur, are you all right?'

'Yes,' I say. 'It's a long story and we haven't got much time to tell it.'

Eventually we persuade the Lost Girls to put their weapons away and to throw ropes down to us.

We climb out of the hole, then, with Stella keeping her eyes glued on Crowky, we make our way across the meadow and on to the beach. We're fairly certain we've got a few hours before the *Alisha* arrives but we want to keep a lookout. We sit in a circle at the bottom of one of the dunes. Mitch piles seaweed over her tail to keep it cool, and Stella and Crowky glare at each other. The air crackles with tension. Crowky burned the Lost Girls' home to the ground and stuffed Stella; in retaliation they stole his beloved Crow's Nest and destroyed most of his scarecrow army. It's fair to say they hate each other's guts.

'Tell us what's going on,' says Stella.

As quickly as possible we explain that some fairies are heading this way, and that one of them, Moss, is planning to do something terrible in Roar. 'Moss is fast, strong and dangerous,' says Rose. 'The moment she sets foot in Roar we have to catch her.'

'So what's the plan?' asks Stella.

We shift uncomfortably. We were so focused on beating Moss back to Roar that we don't actually have a plan. 'Well, first we need to make sure the dragons stay away,' says Rose. 'She can change into any living creature by biting them. She calls it "stealing their skin".'

The Lost Girls' eyes grow a little wider. 'Cool . . .' whispers Audrey, one of the smallest girls.

'I know it sounds cool, but it's not,' says Win. 'What you've got to understand about Moss is that she absolutely *hates* Arthur. If she becomes a dragon, she can do anything she wants to get her revenge on him.'

'Still sounds quite cool,' mutters Audrey.

'Look, I know you say these fairies have got magical powers and stuff,' says Stella, 'but they're small and there are only three of them. When they arrive why don't we just, I don't know, bundle on top of them?'

'*Bundle on top of them?*' They're the first words Crowky has spoken and they're dripping with sarcasm. 'I've seen Moss pull a tree out of the ground and throw it at her sister because she gave me an apple. All the fairies are strong, but Moss is the strongest of them all and she doesn't care who she hurts.'

'So how do we stop them?' asks Stella.

'We can take away their powers,' I say, 'but Rose and I have forgotten how to do it.'

'Well that's helpful,' says Stella, rolling her eyes. 'Why don't we use the dragons?'

Rose shakes her head. 'No, Moss and the dragons can't meet.'

There are a few moments of hopeless silence, then Win jumps to his feet. 'If we work together, then I know we can sort this out! Look how we got rid of Hati Skoll and Crowky – no offence, mate,' he mutters in Crowky's direction. 'In fact, I know exactly what we should do!'

Mitch narrows her eyes. 'Oh yes? And what's that?'

Win's eyes grow wide. 'Make a massive fairy trap!'

CHAPTER 45

Win's fairy trap plan isn't perfect – in Mitch's words it 'stinks like a unicorn's hoof' – but we go along with it because we don't have time to think of an alternative.

We're taking a gamble and assuming that Moss will come ashore on the sandy beach where we crash-landed. It's the obvious place: at the heart of Roar, and free from rocks and cliffs. It's where we brought the *Alisha* when we came back from The End, so we're hoping Moss will do the same.

We're planning to use the Lost Girls' treasure pits. The meadow behind the beach is covered in these deep holes and they're the perfect size to catch a fairy. Mitch will magic up a mist to hide them from view, and the Lost Girls are going to disguise as many of the holes as possible with a layer of twigs and straw. We just have to work out how to get the fairies to fall into one of them.

It's Crowky who thinks of the perfect bait. 'We use Arthur,' he says with a growl.

'Me?' I say. 'Why?'

'Because Moss hates you,' he says with a shrug, 'and if she sees you standing there when you're supposed to be trapped on her island she's going to furious. She's going to want to get hold of you and crush the life out of you!' He squeezes his hands together to demonstrate exactly what he means and his eyes take on a faraway look.

'Yeah . . . I can see how it might work,' I say.

Once we've decided on this plan we divide up the jobs. Mitch will get the ingredients for her mist potion while Stella and the Lost Girls cover the pits. As they're doing this, Rose will call her dragons. 'I'll tell them to go to the Tangled Forest,' she says, 'and not to move a single claw unless they hear my whistle.'

While all this is going on Win will go to the waterfall to fetch the nets he arranged there to stop Crowky from getting into Home. He claims they're made of nymph hair and strong enough to trap a fairy 'for a bit', which has got to be better than nothing.

That leaves me and Crowky.

When we were deciding what to do with Moss once she'd fallen into a pit we hit a problem. We didn't want to hurt her; we just wanted to take her back to her island, but how could we do that? Win's nets might be strong, but they wouldn't keep her trapped for long.

'We need a cage,' says Mitch. 'Something fairy-proof, dragon-proof and magic-proof. Something no one can *ever* escape from.'

Stella laughs. 'Where are we going to get one of those?'

A second later Crowky growls, 'I've got one.'

Of course he has.

He tells us it's hidden at the Crow's Nest, so after a bit of discussion it's agreed that I will go with him on Vlad to bring the cage back to the beach.

So that's my job. Before I get to be living bait for Moss I'm going to babysit Crowky on a trip to the Crow's Nest, the place where he stuffed our grandad and planned to keep me and Rose locked up for life. When I tell Rose I'm not too happy about this, she just shrugs and says, 'Well, this is kind of all your fault, Arthur. You did send the fairies to The End.'

I did. So I accept my fate and, after Rose has called Vlad, Crowky and I set off on the dragon's back to fetch what Crowky calls his 'best cage'.

CHAPTER 46

What Crowky didn't mention about his best cage was how heavy it was or how long it would take him to find it.

'We need to get going!' I shout for the tenth time, my voice echoing up through the Crow's Nest. I'm standing in a huge cold chamber. The last time I was here the Lost Girls made me toast, and I can still see their toasting forks resting in the embers of a long-dead fire. Just when I'm starting to wonder if the whole 'best cage' business was a trick, Crowky appears from a doorway, dragging an ornate cage behind him.

His button eyes don't stop moving. They dart around the inside of the Crow's Nest, taking in the unlit fire and the huge twisting staircase that rises to the top of the castle. The Lost Girls might have spent the summer in the Tangled Forest rebuilding Treetops, but there are still plenty of reminders that they've been living here: a card game is spread out across the floor and scrunchies are looped over the twiggy banister. Crowky's eyes linger on a pile of discarded scarecrow parts scattered by the fireplace. The Lost Girls have been using these as cushions.

His wings tremble. It's bitterly cold in here.

'We should go,' I say, taking one side of the cage.

He grunts and tears his eyes away from the scarecrow arms and legs. Then together we heave the cage towards the castle doors.

It's only when we're standing on the rocks at the foot of the castle, and Vlad is swooping towards us, claws outstretched, that I realise we're going to have to travel back to the beach inside the cage. 'What are you waiting for?' Crowky hisses, holding the door open, and I have no choice but to climb inside.

It's a strange journey back to the beach. Crowky and I sit on opposite sides of the cage that's dangling from Vlad's claws. I keep a tight grip on the bars as, far below us, waves smash against the rocks and cliffs. Despite the cold and Crowky's hard stare, I can't help noticing how beautiful Roar looks. The sun has started to set and the sky is ablaze with colour. The sea a deep velvety blue. I sniff the air and over the smell of salt and Vlad's fiery breath, I pick up a trace of marzipan . . . Magic!

'Mitch must have cast her spell,' I say.

On the other side of the cage Crowky sniffs deeply. 'Oh, that's magic all right,' he says, 'but it isn't Mitch's. Moss must be getting close.'

'Fobastober!' I call to Vlad and we soar on through the golden sky.

***

Vlad carefully drops the cage in the middle of the meadow and we step out into chaos. The Lost Girls are scurrying around, disguising the holes with anything they can find, and Mitch is busy crushing shells and mashing seaweed and tipping them into a bubbling cauldron. 'I'm making the mist nice and low,' she says as a dense white cloud billows over the side of the cauldron. 'I want to make sure Moss can spot you.'

Great.

Now Vlad is back Rose can finally get rid of the dragons.

She stands on the beach with all three of them gathered round her. It's a strange sight. Rose is wearing her ripped and burnt onesie and the dragons are huffing and puffing in her face. I watch as she scratches their snouts and as they nuzzle her back. They seem particularly interested in her stone and keep dipping their heads to sniff at it. Smoke pours from their gaping mouths and mingles with Mitch's spreading mist. It looks like Rose is finding it hard to send them away, and I can understand that – it feels safe with them close by – but they have to go.

Rose starts whispering to them in Obby Dobby and gets a lick from Bad Dragon's crusty black tongue. For a moment she disappears completely in a cloud of sparks and smoke. Then, with Bad Dragon taking the lead, the three dragons turn and start galloping across the beach. The ground shakes, their wings stretch out and then they're rising up into the sky and heading towards the safety of the Tangled Forest.

Rose watches them go then walks over to me. 'Come on,' she says, taking my arm. 'It's time to catch a fairy.'

CHAPTER 47

I'm standing in the middle of a sea of mist. It spreads away from me like a blanket that hides everything. Somewhere up ahead waves crash. I can hear them but I can't see them. I can't see the pit either, but I know it's in front of me, deep and steep-sided. It's the largest one the Lost Girls made and right now it's covered with a thin layer of twigs, rushes and grass.

Crouched down somewhere behind me are Win, Rose and Crowky. The Lost Girls are nearby too, scattered across the meadow and holding Win's nets, just in case Moss refuses to take the bait and walks in the wrong direction. Mitch is out at sea looking for the *Alisha*. The moment she spots it she's going to throw a potion up in the air and a crash of thunder will echo through the sky.

Our trap is set.

For a while it actually feels good standing here. We've beaten Moss back to Roar and we're ready for her!

But as the minutes tick by, and the cold mist wraps round

me, I start to feel very alone. I know my friends are close by, but the silence and the mist do strange things to my mind. I imagine Moss slipping past Mitch and creeping up on me. I picture her grabbing hold of my leg and pulling me down.

A rumble of thunder crashes through the sky. I jump and my chest squeezes tight.

She's coming.

I stare straight ahead, desperately trying to see or hear something. Then I spot the looming shape of the *Alisha*. How long will it take Moss to get to shore? Not long, I think, remembering how fast she can row.

Minutes tick by. Nothing happens.

Then, just as I'm wondering if our whole plan has failed, three shadowy figures rise out of the mist, silhouetted against the setting sun. Not one fairy but three. Of course Moss would bring her brothers. Whatever she's got planned she'll use their magic too.

The figures walk towards me. I thought the fairies would be bickering, or chatting, excited to be in Roar, but they are totally silent. They move forward. Stop. Then start walking again. Now they've reached the meadow, but they've turned and are walking in the wrong direction!

I know what I have to do.

'MOSS!'

My voice shatters the silence and makes the fairies spin round. I wave my arms high above my head and I jump up and down. 'Moss, I'm over here!'

I hear a scream of anger and the fairy leading the way – Moss, I'm guessing – grabs hold of the other two and pulls them towards me. They move fast, scuttling like spiders.

'*Arthur Trout!*' Moss's voice is hard and angry. 'What are *you* doing here?' I fight the urge to run as she drags her brothers closer. They come to a stop and I try to work out if they've reached the pit. The sun is so low I can barely see a thing. *Come closer*, I think. *Come closer!*

The fairies take a step . . . then another. 'Get him!' cries Moss, but before they can move there is a crack, a surprised yelp, and the three fairies disappear from sight.

CHAPTER 48

'Come on, Arthur!' Rose shouts, pulling me forward. Win and Crowky follow, dragging a net behind them. We stop at the edge of the pit, but we can't see a thing. It's filled to the brim with the same mist that's spread across the beach and meadow.

'Are they down there?' asks Win.

'Must be,' I say. 'I saw them fall.'

We hear a yell followed by frantic scrabbling sounds. I hold my breath, half expecting Moss to shoot out and launch herself at me. But nothing happens and soon the scrabbling stops. Our pit has worked. The fairies are trapped!

One by one, the Lost Girls join us, keen to catch their first glimpse of a fairy. Sophie throws a stick into the swirling mist and a moment later it shoots back narrowly missing her face. 'Whoa!' she says, a look of fear and delight on her face.

Rose nudges me. 'We've caught them. Now what do we do?'

I'm not entirely sure. We were so focused on setting our

trap that we didn't think about how we'd get the fairies into the cage. 'We wait for the mist to go,' I say, trying to sound confident. 'Then, when we can see the fairies, we throw a net down, pull them out and shove them in the cage.'

Rose nods and we go back to staring into the pit.

Then something strange happens. A long, low whistle comes drifting out of the mist-filled hole. I recognise it immediately. It's the whistle Rose uses to summon her dragons, only Rose isn't whistling. She's standing next to me, looking as confused as I am.

The sound gets louder, sending a shiver down my spine.

'Look!' Win nudges me. 'The mist is clearing!'

Mitch's spell must be wearing off because all around us the mist is breaking up, revealing patches of meadow and sea. Down in the pit I spot three little figures. Straight away I see Moss's tangle of blonde hair. I'm expecting her to look furious, but instead when she gazes up at me she smiles. Her hand is wrapped round Owl's neck. He's trying to peel her fingers off one by one, but it's impossible. She's too strong.

'Oh no . . .' whispers Rose, and that's when I see who the third fairy is.

It should be Twig – who else could it be? – but this fairy has a long plait draped over her shoulder, and her face is lifted up to the sky and she's whistling.

'Pebble?' hisses Crowky. 'What are you doing?'

'She's calling a dragon for me!' cries Moss.

Almost as soon as the words are out of her mouth we

hear the *thud*, *thud*, *thud* of beating wings and a ball of fire explodes in the sky. Moss gives a yelp of joy and jumps up and down.

It's Bad Dragon. Her huge silhouette appears against the setting sun and her wings pound the air as she rushes to get to Rose.

'*That's* Pebble's secret power!' I say, remembering the fish that surrounded her in the sea and the parrots that flew down to perch on her shoulder. 'She can call creatures to her!'

'Any creatures at all,' says Moss, 'so when you told me about your mighty dragons I knew we had to take a detour to pick her up.'

'And we told you exactly where she was,' I say.

'I know!' Moss laughs. 'It's so funny!'

As we've been talking, Pebble continues to whistle, drawing Bad Dragon even closer.

'Pebble, please, stop it!' begs Rose, but Pebble ignores her and carries on whistling, her chest rising and falling with the effort.

'She won't stop because of Owl,' snarls Crowky. 'Look, Moss is hurting him!'

Moss squeezes Owl's neck even tighter. She's whispering in his ear too and suddenly his hands shoot up in the air and his fingers start wriggling.

We know what this means: he's making a storm. Wind bursts out of the pit, knocking us backwards. It whirls above our heads before whipping across the meadow, making a path through the remaining mist and the grass. It shoots across the beach, sending sand flying in all directions, and rushes out to sea. All is still for a moment, then the wind races back towards us, bringing the sea with it.

'Is it working?' cries Moss. She can't see what's happening from down in the pit, but she can tell from our faces that something is going on. The wave Owl has made gets bigger and bigger as it hurtles towards land. The Lost Girls shift uneasily as it picks up speed. Could it really come all the way up the beach and reach us here in the meadow?

We have to do something . . .

'Crowky, Win!' I shout. 'Throw the net!' They heave the net over their heads and down into the hole. It lands on the fairies, knocking Moss to the ground. For a brief moment the whistling stops and Owl's wave slows down, but then Moss is on her feet and grabbing her brother and sister, and their magic starts again.

The wave reaches the beach and rushes up the sand. Above us Bad Dragon growls and sparks shower down on us.

'What are you going to do?' I shout to Moss. 'Turn into Bad Dragon and burn down Roar? Why?'

Moss pokes her face through the net. 'Because you love Roar, Arthur, that's why!'

'But you'll destroy your home!' I say.

She stares at me. 'I don't care about this place. I've got plans, Arthur Trout!'

'Plans?' I say. 'What do you mean?'

She grins and I see her sharp teeth. 'I'll give you a clue,' she says, then she squawks three times. She sounds just like a parrot.

'She's bonkers!' says Win.

'Oh, and, Arthur,' says Moss, 'don't forget that I still have this!' She puffs out her chest showing us Grandad's torn 'NO PROB-LLAMA!' T-shirt.

I'm frozen. I don't know what to do. I want to scramble into the pit and try to get the T-shirt, but I can't because Owl's wave has just crashed over the sand dunes and is racing towards us.

'RUN!' screams Stella, and the Lost Girls scatter in all directions. Pebble's whistling gets louder and Bad Dragon dives towards the hole, desperately looking for Rose. Fire pours from her gaping jaws and Rose jumps up and down, shouting, 'Gobo obawobay!' but in the chaos of the mist and the approaching wave, Bad Dragon can't see Rose. She thinks she can hear her, though, because Pebble is whistling louder than ever.

Bad Dragon hovers above us, her huge tail lashing back and forth. Then the wave reaches us. It surges round the hole, knocking Stella to the ground.

'STOP WHISTLING, Pebble!' cries Crowky. 'I won't let Moss hurt you or your brother!'

Miraculously the whistling stops. Bad Dragon rears up in confusion, and that's when her tail dips into the hole.

Moss lets go of her brother and sister, leaps in the air and sinks her teeth into Bad Dragon's hard scales.

And that's when the wave hits us.

CHAPTER 49

I tumble round and round under water as I'm dragged back across the meadow by the wave. Just when I feel like my lungs might burst my head breaks the surface and I take a mouthful of air before I'm pulled under again.

I try not to struggle. I let myself be pulled with the wave until I can stick my head up and grab another breath of air. This time I catch a glimpse of Bad Dragon thrashing in the sky before the swirling water throws me against a rock. I dig my nails into a crack and hold on as the wave rushes on without me.

But Owl must have stopped making the wind driving the wave because suddenly it slows down, then begins to roll back the way it just came. It charges past me, trying to take me with it, but I cling on to the rock and soon the wave has returned to the sea leaving the meadow a mess of branches, flattened sunflowers and water-filled holes.

My whole body is shaking as I prise my fingers off the rock and stand up.

All across the meadow figures are picking themselves up from where the wave dumped them. I spot Crowky and Rose scrambling out of a tree and Win crawling on his hands and knees towards the pit where, minutes ago, Moss bit Bad Dragon's tail. It's now filled to the brim with muddy water. Moss pulls herself out. She doesn't seem tired at all. She jumps to her feet and stares up at the sky where Bad Dragon is twisting and turning.

Pebble and Owl are still splashing in the water trying to reach the side. Bad Dragon growls, sending a blast of fire across the meadow. Sparks shower down over Moss, but she doesn't even flinch.

I stumble forward. Somehow I've got to stop Moss from changing into Bad Dragon. I'm aching all over from smacking into the rock, but I force myself to run. I reach the pit just as Moss's body starts to shimmer.

'NO!' I shout as Moss lifts her hands to her face and the shimmering transfers to Bad Dragon. The dragon's leathery wings tremble and the fire billowing from her mouth looks like a flickering film. Then, without warning, she drops from the sky, straight towards the pit and Owl and Pebble.

Win realises what's about to happen and jumps into the water. He grabs hold of Owl and Pebble's shoulders and heaves them out of the way before Bad Dragon's body slams down. A muddy wave throws them all out of the pit, dumping them by my feet.

Bad Dragon has collapsed with her belly in the pit and

her head and tail stretched across the meadow. She's stopped shimmering and looks solid again. Her eyes start to close and a single puff of smoke escapes from her nostrils.

There is a blinding flash of light. When I look up Moss has vanished and there's a new dragon up in the sky. This one looks just like the creature slumped in the pit. She has red eyes, armoured scales and sharp spikes marching down her spine. But this isn't Bad Dragon. It's Moss dressed in her stolen skin.

Rose runs to my side, mud dripping from her torn onesie. 'Is that Moss?'

I nod. 'We need to get everyone away from here!'

The Moss-dragon pounds her wings, testing out their power. Then she shoots up in the sky, twists into a dive, and plunges towards us.

'RUN!' Rose shouts across the meadow.

As the dragon races to earth everyone scatters. Luckily Stella has trained the Lost Girls to act quickly. They split up, some heading towards the sand dunes, others for the banks of the Rainbow River. Win drags Pebble and Owl away from the pit towards a patch of trees.

That leaves me, Rose and Crowky . . . and the dragon.

It's me Moss hates. I need to lead her away from the others, not towards them. Rose has obviously decided to stay with me. I don't know why Crowky's still here.

The dragon growls. It's a terrible sound. It makes the insides of my body shake.

It's Crowky who moves first. He starts to run across the meadow, snarling, 'Follow me!'

Rose and I do what he says, following as he leaps across muddy pits and dodges piles of wood and seaweed. Of course, Crowky can use his wings to help him jump and soon Rose and I fall behind, but we see where he's going: towards a Jenga-like stack of rocks.

I slip in the mud and Rose hauls me to my feet. I don't look back but I can feel the heat from the dragon's flames and hear the thud of her wings as she catches up with us.

Crowky reaches the rocks and crawls into a hole at the bottom of the stack.

'Come on, Arthur!' shouts Rose.

She's always been a faster runner than me, but she won't leave me behind. When my lungs feel like they might burst she grabs my T-shirt and pulls me forward.

The rocks are close now, but so is the dragon.

Rose glances back and her eyes widen with fear. I know I shouldn't, but I look back too.

The dragon is right behind us, flying with her belly low to the ground. Her jaws snap open and her talons reach for me. Then the fire comes.

It shoots forward, brushing the backs of my legs.

Rose reaches the rocks, throws herself to the ground and rolls inside. I'm nearly there. I can see the gap. I force my legs to move faster, and that's when I trip and slam down. The dragon's shadow falls over me. There is stink of sulphur, a snarl, but just as the flames lick my feet, hands land on my shoulders and drag me to safety.

Rose and Crowky pull me deeper and deeper into the cave until there is nowhere else to go. A ball of fire follows us, scurries along the walls, creeping closer. I shut my eyes and feel a wave of heat. It's over in a second and when I open my eyes the fire has gone.

Then there is silence.

CHAPTER 50

I turn away from the opening and look at Rose and Crowky. They stare back at me with wide eyes and I realise that for the first time in my life I'm not scared of Crowky.

'That was close,' I say.

Rose laughs and shakes her head. 'I can't believe you tripped, Arthur!'

'I can,' rasps Crowky.

This makes Rose laugh even louder and because I'm so happy that I didn't just get toasted by a dragon, I laugh too.

Crowky watches us through narrowed eyes until we stop laughing. Then Rose leads us towards the entrance of the cave. Cautiously we poke out heads out.

The Moss-dragon is far away, twisting in the sky over the Bottomless Ocean and roaring with all her might. The sky is on fire. Bad Dragon is still collapsed in the pit while her mirror image flies above her, burning whatever she can see.

We crawl out and watch as flames stream from the dragon's jaws, obliterating what's left of the meadow. A row of sunflowers disintegrates in seconds and a lone tree explodes in a ball of fire. The air is filled with smoke and the dragon's wild screams.

There is one glimmer of hope: she seems to have forgotten about us hidden away by this stack of rocks. We watch helplessly as she shoots out over the sea and sets fire to the *Alisha*'s sails. They burn brightly against the dark sky and I see the orangutans leap up to the rigging.

'What are they doing?' I say.

'Cutting the sails down,' replies Rose.

A burning sail plummets to the deck, but before the wooden boards can catch alight the orangutans bundle it overboard where it sinks beneath the waves.

Luckily the Moss-dragon doesn't see the orangutans

saving the *Alisha*. Now she's circling the meadow, burning the last remaining sunflowers. Then, with a flick of her tail, she shoots inland, following the curves of the Rainbow River.

'Where's she going?' asks Rose.

'That river leads to the On-Off Waterfall,' growls Crowky.

'And that leads to Home,' I say.

Rose grabs my arm. 'Arthur, when you were with her in the jungle, and you thought she was me, are you sure you didn't tell her that the T-shirt would let her into Home?'

'I'm certain,' I say.

She turns to Crowky. 'What about you? Did you tell her?'

He scowls. 'I'd never do something so stupid.'

Rose looks at me. 'That thing she said when she squawked like a parrot. That she had 'plans'. What do you think she meant?'

'I don't know,' I say, desperately, 'but Win's taken down all his nets and she has the T-shirt so there's nothing to stop her from getting into Home.'

I think about Grandad alone in his house. It's evening now. He'll be sitting at his kitchen table, a cup of tea in front of him along with the biscuit tin and a carefully cut-out crossword puzzle. Then I remember what Moss said when I was trapped in the cave with Crowky: *I'm going to steal something from you, Arthur. Something you love . . .*

'Rose,' I say, 'what if Grandad is the thing Moss is going to steal from me?'

Her eyes widen. 'We need to go back to Home. Now!'

'Take me with you,' growls Crowky.

'What?' I say.

'You can't do anything to stop Moss. You have no magical powers. You're weak. You need these!' He shoves his stick fingers in front of my face.

Does Crowky really want to help, or is this a trick to finally get into Home? His sack face gives nothing away. The wind whistles across the still-burning meadow, sending sparks up into the air. I hear a growl followed by a heavy thud. Bad Dragon has rolled out of the pit. Her tail slams against the ground as she tries to stand up.

'You haven't got much time,' hisses Crowky. 'Moss is back in her body!'

'Come on,' says Rose, grabbing hold of Crowky's arm and then mine. She marches us towards Bad Dragon. 'We're going to Home. All of us.'

But when we reach the dragon, we find she can barely stand up, let alone fly. While Rose whispers in her ear, urging her to get to her feet, the Lost Girls appear in ones and twos and Win runs over with Pebble and Owl.

'Crowky!' It's the first word I've ever heard Pebble speak and she shouts it with joy as she hurls herself into his arms.

Stella, Win and I stare in amazement as Pebble clings to his straw-stuffed body. He looks as surprised as we are and stands there for a moment, arms stiff, before giving her a pat and saying with a growl, 'I have to go.'

Pebble looks distraught. 'Where?'

'To stop Moss. She's going to do something bad.' Pebble nods; she understands. 'But I'll come back. Soon.'

Bad Dragon's head is drooping, but she's on her feet and cautiously stretching her wings. Quickly we tell Stella and Win where we're going.

Win's horrified. 'You can't take him and not me!' he says, shooting a look in Crowky's direction.

'We need his hands,' I say. 'Rose and I can't stop Moss on our own.'

'But I can do magic. I can help you!' he protests.

'We need you here,' I say, and it's true. I explain that someone has to check that Twig is on the *Alisha* and that the orangutans and Mitch are OK. Plus we need him to keep an eye on the fairies.

'So what you're saying is that you need a powerful ninja wizard to protect Roar,' he says, nodding seriously. 'Got it.'

'And I need you to look after this,' says Rose, and she

takes the net bag holding her stone-egg and hangs it round Win's neck.

He gazes down at it. 'Really?' he says.

Rose nods. 'Take good care of it. I think it's going to hatch soon.'

'Good luck,' shouts Win as the three of us clamber on Bad Dragon's back. 'Bring me back some rocky road!'

Bad Dragon stretches her wings and starts to lumber across the burnt meadow. Rose leans over her neck. 'When all this is over we'll meet at Mitch's island!' she shouts to Stella and Win.

Then Bad Dragon takes a leap forward, thrusts down her wings and we lift up in the sky. As we rise higher, I look around, taking in the damage Moss has inflicted during her rampage as Bad Dragon. Fire has broken out across the Tangled Forest and meadows have been razed to the ground. I can see a thick plume of smoke rising from the

Bad Side and wonder what's burning there. Could it be the Crow's Nest?

Moss did all this to punish me. Whatever she's got planned next, we have to stop her.

CHAPTER 51

I've never seen Rose fly a dragon so fast.

Bad Dragon's wings crash up and down as we hurtle towards the On-Off Waterfall. Cool wind rushes past my face and the dragon's fiery breath lights up the darkness that surrounds us. Night has fallen properly now and we're flying by the light of the moon. I cling to a spike, my fingers cold and numb. I feel numb inside too, knowing Moss could already be walking through Grandad's house.

'Fobastober!' cries Rose, rubbing Bad Dragon's neck. 'Fobastober!'

Soon we hear the rumble and crash of the On-Off Waterfall.

Rose is planning to guide Bad Dragon to the ledge, but we don't make it that far. Worn out from when Moss stole her skin, Bad Dragon suddenly drops lower in the sky. Her trailing tail hits trees as she desperately looks for somewhere to land.

We cling on as she tips left and then right before crashing down in the meadow. The three of us tumble into long grass. Leaving Bad Dragon slumped across the ground we pick ourselves up and run into the forest. It's pitch-black – the moon can't reach through the thick trees – but Crowky seems to know the way and we follow him.

Rose must trip on something because suddenly she yells and slams to the ground. She rolls on her back, clutching her ankle and gasping with pain. 'I've twisted it,' she says. 'Or worse.'

I help her to her feet, but the moment she tries to walk she falls down again. Ahead we can see the pool at the bottom of the On-Off Waterfall. In the moonlight it looks like a circle of silver. The cliff looms up behind it. It's steep, and we know that the rocky steps are covered in grease. There's no way Rose is going to be able to climb up there. Panic rises inside me. Moss could be in Grandad's house!

'Go,' Rose says through gritted teeth. 'You and Crowky . . . go to Home, find Moss and stop whatever she's got planned!'

I can see Crowky waiting at the edge of the forest, a silent, brooding figure. His wings open then snap shut.

'But what about you? I can't leave you here in the forest.'

She grabs hold of my hand and squeezes it. 'You have to go, Arthur. *Now!*' There's something desperate about the way she says this that makes me hesitate. Rose and I are twins. She often knows what I'm thinking, but it doesn't

272

usually work the other way round. But right now I can tell she's keeping something from me.

'What is it, Rose? Tell me.'

'I think I've worked out why Moss squawked like a parrot,' she says, shaking her head, 'and if I'm right . . .'

'Just tell me!' I say.

'Moss knows how to get into Home because *you* told her.'

'I didn't!' I protest.

'Yes, you did, Arthur. Remember when Mitch disappeared? We were on the beach and you started talking about the T-shirt.'

I think back. It was dark on the beach and we were waiting for the fairies to get back so we could start looking for Mitch. 'But Moss wasn't there,' I say. 'She'd gone to check her lighthouse.'

'But she *was* there. Remember the green parrot that kept me awake? That was Moss!'

She's right! The parrot's shrill cry sounded exactly like the sound Moss made in the pit! A horrible feeling runs through me as I remember what else I talked about that night.

'Moss knows about the camp bed,' I say. 'She knows what will happen if anyone opens it . . .'

'That's why you've got to go, Arthur!' says Rose, desperately. 'Any second now Moss could open that bed and you, me, Win, Mitch, everything –' she snaps her fingers in front of my face – 'will be gone!'

CHAPTER 52

Everything gone. Panic presses down on my chest until it hurts.

'Rose, why didn't you tell me?' I say.

'I only worked it out when we were flying here on Bad Dragon, and I didn't tell you because I knew *this* would happen.' She squeezes my hand and that's when I realise that my whole body is trembling.

Rose is right, of course. I'm so scared that I'm frozen to the spot, a useless, shaking mess. Why am I even standing here? It's my fault all this has happened. I have to get to Home and stop Moss!

I turn to go, but Rose tightens her grip on my hand. 'Find the Fairy Fact File, Arthur. It will tell you how we can take away her powers. That's the only way you can stop her!'

I pull away and run through the forest.

'You can do this, Arthur!' Rose calls after me. 'Remember, you're a Master of Roar!'

But I don't feel like a Master of Roar, I feel hopeless,

stupid, and when I reach Crowky I'm dizzy with panic. 'We need to get in that tunnel,' I say. 'Now!'

He nods, but before I can start climbing the cliff face, his wings spring open and he grabs hold of my shoulders and he lifts me up in the air. His wings work hard. Feathers fall to the ground, but he keeps going, occasionally using his feet to push us higher up the cliff until we reach the ledge outside the tunnel.

He throws me down then hunches over, taking great gasping breaths. He stretches out his stick fingers, then curls them up one by one.

'Thank you,' I say.

He glares at me from under his messy straw hair. 'I did that for *me*. Moss has to be stopped.'

I nod. He's right. Quickly I pull off a trainer and hand it to him. 'This will let you into Home. Sorry,' I say, risking a smile. 'It probably smells.'

He stares at my battered trainer as if he can't quite believe his eyes. 'It's a key,' he whispers, 'like the T-shirt.' Slowly he looks up at me. We both know that if he wanted to he could throw me off this cliff and go into Roar alone. But he doesn't. 'Go!' he says, pushing me ahead of him into the tunnel.

I crawl into the darkness, the sound of rustling feathers and straw telling me that Crowky is behind me. I go as fast as I can. My knees scrape against rocks and my head bangs the roof of the tunnel.

'She'll be hard to stop.' Crowky's whisper echoes around me.

'I know,' I say, 'We have to take away her powers.'

A moment later Crowky says, 'She's going to do something to your grandad.'

His words made me freeze for a moment. I've been so worried about Moss opening the bed that I'd forgotten about Grandad. 'How can you be so sure?'

After a pause he says, 'Moss and me . . . we think alike. If I was going to steal something you love, that's what I'd take.'

And what you did take, I think, as I feel soft mattress under my hands, but I don't say another word because if Moss is in the attic we can't let her know that we're coming.

I crawl forward and slowly stick my head out of the folded mattress.

The overhead light is on and I can see that the room is empty. I pull myself out of the bed and on to the attic floor.

The door leading to the stairs is standing open and the room is a mess. Our toys have been tipped out of their trunk and Prosecco is lying on his side. Grandad's chess set is scattered across the floor and I can see the 'NO PROB-LLAMA!' T-shirt dumped by the door. Moss has obviously been here.

Although I want to run straight out of the room and find Grandad, I force myself to look for the Fairy Fact File. Quickly I search through the mess on the floor. I find dressing-up clothes, plastic dragons and cuddly toys, but none of our pictures or stories. Where could it be?

A scuffle makes me turn round.

Crowky is crawling out of the mattress. This is something I've imagined over and over again, and now it's actually happening. He pulls his shoulders out, then his legs and jumps to his feet. His wings burst open. He looks around

with wide unblinking eyes.

'So this is it?' he says. 'Home . . .'

He starts to prowl around the room, his wings brushing the floor, and that's when I smell smoke.

I run to the window. Grandad is having a bonfire! The sight of him sitting in a deckchair, a stick in one hand and a mug in the other, makes me cry out with relief. His hair is as messy as ever and, of course, he's wearing shorts. His feet are bare and stretched towards the glowing wood. I'm about to throw open the window and call his name when I see something else. Standing behind him, half hidden by a tree, is Moss.

Grandad hasn't got a clue that she's there.

Moss stares at him intently, her face lit up by the flames of the bonfire.

Fear runs through me. It squeezes my stomach and makes my mouth go dry. Crowky stands by my side. 'I can see her,' I whisper. Then I push past him and run out of the attic.

CHAPTER 53

I take the stairs two at a time with Crowky following close behind. 'What are you going to do?' he hisses. 'Run out there and grab hold of her? She'll throw you into the fire!'

I know Crowky's right. I know that really I should keep looking for the Fairy Fact File, check in the spare bedroom where Grandad keeps boxes of junk, but I'm too desperate to get to Grandad.

I run through the kitchen and see the back door standing open. Before I can rush outside Crowky yanks me back. 'We can't let her know we're here,' he snarls. 'We'd lose the only advantage we've got!'

I nod. Then, in silence, we step outside. The bonfire crackles. Moonlight fills the garden. Out on the road a car goes past and the sound is so surprising it makes me jump. Crowky's hand tightens round my arm, keeping me still. We creep as close as we dare then crouch behind a bush. Crowky's straw stuffing is alarmingly rustly, but Moss doesn't turn round. She's transfixed.

Grandad's sipping his drink when Moss steps out of the shadows.

'Hello,' she says, her little voice ringing out in the quiet of the garden. 'Are you Grandad?'

Grandad is startled and sloshes tea over his knees. He gets up and peers at Moss. 'Who are you?' he says.

'Moss,' she says, smiling up at him, 'and I've come from Roar.'

Confusion flashes over Grandad's face, but once he's got over the surprise of seeing a fairy in his garden, he doesn't look worried at all. Who would be worried by a sweet little girl with big eyes and leaves in her hair?

'What are you doing here?' he says with a chuckle. 'Did you take a wrong turn in that tunnel and end up in my attic?' He's so calm that he takes a sip of what's left of his tea, then adds, 'Where are my manners? Would you like something to drink? There's more tea in the pot, and I've got biscuits too.'

Moss shakes her head shyly. 'No thank you. There's no time. Arthur and Rose sent me. Something bad has happened to them.' The smile vanishes from Grandad's face as Moss carries on. 'That scarecrow got them so I came to find you.'

What's she playing at? I thought Moss might be about to use her magic to hurt Grandad in some way, but it sounds like she wants to take him back to Roar. She reaches out a small hand. 'Please come with me. We've got to be quick.'

Flustered now, Grandad nods. 'Yes, of course. Let me

put out the fire.' He reaches for a watering can. I'm about to jump up and warn him not to go anywhere with Moss when Crowky pulls me back. He shakes his head and points towards the house. He wants me to go inside.

The moment we're in the kitchen he hisses, 'You can't let her know we're here! That fairy has torn my arms off my body more times than I can remember. We need a plan!'

I glance over my shoulder. The fire is smouldering and Moss is leading Grandad by the hand across the garden. They're coming straight towards us.

'Listen,' I whisper. 'Somewhere in this house is a booklet Rose made: the Fairy Fact File. If we find it, we'll know how to take away the fairies' powers.'

Crowky snarls, 'Where is it?'

'I don't know! There's a spare room where Grandad keeps stuff. It could be in there.'

So as Moss and Grandad walk towards the back door we slip out of the kitchen and back upstairs. Crowky and I bundle into the spare room. There are boxes piled from floor to ceiling.

'What's in the box?' whispers Crowky.

I stare at him. Did he just make a joke? If he did, he isn't smiling. Downstairs I hear Grandad say to Moss, 'Do I need to bring anything? Plasters? Water? Maybe a thermos of hot squash?'

'Nothing,' says Moss. 'They just need you.'

I turn back to the boxes. Luckily they're all labelled. Most have boring stuff like CAR and INSURANCE written on them, but one has a picture of me and Rose stuck on the front. I pull off the lid and turn it upside down. Photos, pictures and handmade cards spill across the carpet.

'Quiet!' hisses Crowky.

I freeze. Moss is hurrying Grandad up the stairs. I can hear him struggling to breathe – he needs a puff on his asthma inhaler – and Moss is chattering away.

'Rose and Arthur said you would come straight away. They said, "Find our grandad and get him to come." They said, "He'll be able to help!"'

'But what's happened to them?' asks Grandad.

'*Crowky* is what's happened to them,' says Moss. 'He's so mean!'

Next to me, Crowky sucks in his breath.

'I should never have let them go!' Grandad cries.

He sounds so distressed that I want to run to him, but Crowky puts a hand on my shoulder and squeezes. Moss and Grandad pass the spare room and start to climb the stairs to the attic.

'Whatever she's about to do, I need to stop her!' I whisper to Crowky.

He pulls me close. 'Well, you can't, Arthur Trout, not unless you can take away her powers, so you'd better find that book!'

I desperately sift through the pile of stuff on the floor. Crowky opens a Christmas card I made for Grandad and a robin pops out at him. I flick through drawings of cars, castles, dragons and monsters, but I can't see Rose's booklet anywhere.

A heavy thud comes from the attic. It sounds like someone has fallen. Without stopping to think I drop the pictures and run into the corridor. I don't bother sneaking up the stairs. I take them two at a time, slam the door open and burst into the attic. Moss is standing next to the bed, but Grandad is already crawling inside. Only his bare feet stick out.

'NO!' I yell.

I open my mouth, but before I can say anything, Moss has hurled herself across the room and slammed her hands into my chest. I stagger backwards then fall down the stairs. I land in a painful heap. Everything spins as I pick myself up and drag myself back into the attic, but when I get there Grandad has gone.

Moss is back by the bed. She stretches her fingers wide and jumps up and down with excitement. 'You weren't supposed to be here, Arthur,' she says, 'but it's going to be so much better this way!' Then she puts her little hands on each side of the bed, ready to pull it open.

CHAPTER 54

I run forward, but Moss knocks me back with a flick of her hand. I hit the wall so hard that a picture falls on top of me. Before I've even tried to stand up Moss dashes over and grabs my arms. 'I'm not going to let you ruin everything!' she says, shaking me, then she bangs me back into the wall with such force that the room spins. I feel sick and have to shut my eyes for a second. When I open them Moss is still staring down at me. 'Now you stay here!' she says, then, with a sly smile, she backs towards the camp bed.

I swallow. 'What are you going to do?'

Her smile gets bigger. 'I think you know, Arthur Trout. You stole something from me, so now I'm going to steal something from you!' Once again she grabs hold of the bed.

I can't let her open it. Except for Mum and Dad, everything I love is inside that camp bed! But why would Moss care about that? Horror sweeps through me as I desperately try to think of something, *anything* that will stop her.

'Don't!' I say. 'What about your brothers and Pebble?'

She shrugs. 'What about them?'

'If you open that bed, then you will never, *ever* see them again!'

She looks confused. 'So? I never *want* to see them again. They're stupid and they're always ruining my plans. When I got rid of Pebble I should have got rid of Twig and Owl at the same time!'

Clearly Moss doesn't care about anyone except herself. 'What about Roar?' I say. 'It's your home.'

Her face screws up with bitterness. 'It's a rubbish home. I hate it!'

Suddenly a muffled voice calls out from inside the bed. 'Arthur? Are you there?'

It's Rose. She's crawling through the tunnel towards us!

Moss giggles and claps her hands. 'This is perfect!'

As I struggle to my feet, Moss tightens her grip on the bed, but she doesn't open it. She just stands there with a happy smile on her face and I realise that she's waiting for Rose to get closer.

I see a flicker of movement in the doorway. Crowky is standing there, but Moss hasn't noticed him. He puts a finger to his lips and points to the floor by my feet.

I look down. I'm surrounded by splinters of glass and wood from the smashed picture frame. Then I see what was *inside* the frame. It's a little booklet and drawn on the front is a picture of a fairy. She has blonde hair and emerald-green eyes and written above her in Rose's handwriting are the words 'Fairy Fact File'.

'Arthur?' Rose's voice is louder now. She's nearly at the end of the tunnel. '*Arthur, are you there?*'

I pull the fact file out from the glass and open it. Words swim in front of my eyes. 'Fairies are vengeful . . . Fairies make good cakes . . .' I see a picture of Pebble with arrows pointing to all the birds and animals that surround her. Then in a red box I see the words 'IMPORTANT!!! GETTING RID OF FAIRY POWERS' and I read what's written below.

'Arthur?' yells Rose.

I look up and Moss's hands tighten on the bed. '*Never cross a fairy, Arthur!*' she says.

Finally I know how to stop her. But if it's going to work, I have to get close to Rose.

'Arthur?' shouts Rose again. '*Crowky?*'

The second he hears his name, Crowky jumps out from the doorway and launches himself at Moss. He crashes into her and they roll to the ground. Moss kicks him away and he hits a bookshelf. But he's given me the chance I need. I run towards the bed. 'ROSE!' I yell, shoving my hand into the mattress.

Moss spins round and screams as I find Rose's hand and feel her fingers wrap round mine. Moss runs across the room, jumps on my back and grabs the bed. I try to shake her off but she's too strong. 'HEAR ME ROAR!' I shout to Rose.

Moss yanks at the bed.

'HEAR ME ROAR!' Rose's voice echoes back to me.

There is a rusty squeal of springs and an explosion of light bursts out of the gaping mattress. It hits me in the chest sending me and Moss flying backwards. I crash to the ground and Moss rolls off my back. There is a loud ringing in my ears and everything is blurred, but I can see that the bed is closed. Moss is lying next to me. Suddenly she jumps to her feet, ready to race back to the bed. My hand shoots out and I grab her ankle. I brace myself, ready to be kicked or thrown across the room, but Moss just twists frantically.

'Get off me!' she cries. 'I'm warning you, Arthur Trout, you let go of me or I'll bite you!'

But I don't let go of her. I keep my hand on her ankle and I don't let go even when she twists her head round and sinks her teeth into my arm. It hurts. It's definitely worse than a hamster bite, but I grit my teeth and put up with the pain until Crowky pulls her off me and holds her in the air with her arms pinned to her sides.

She twists and kicks out and snarls with annoyance, but she doesn't start to shimmer and neither do I. Her powers are gone. For now she's just a very small, very angry fairy.

I stagger to the bed. I rest my hands on it desperately hoping that everyone inside is still there and is safe. 'It didn't open, did it?' I ask. 'Not properly?'

'No,' says Crowky, 'not properly,' but we both know that it did open, just for a second.

I want to crawl straight into the bed, find Rose and go back to Roar, but first we have to get rid of Moss.

'How did you do it?' Crowky asks, nodding at the Fairy Fact File still clutched in my hand.

I find the right page and read Rose's words out loud: 'Fairies are super powerful, but if the Masters of Roar hold hands and shout "HEAR ME ROAR!!!" they will lose their powers for TEN WHOLE MINUTES.'

Moss thrashes in Crowky's hands, hissing and spitting.

I really wish Rose had written *for ever*.

CHAPTER 55

'Get your horrible twig fingers off me!' screams Moss.
'We've not got much time,' Crowky says. 'What shall we do with her?'

Already several minutes have passed since Rose and I took away Moss's powers.

'I know a place where she won't hurt anyone,' I say.

With Crowky's help I wrap Nani's sari round the wriggling Moss and we drag her, still kicking, towards the door, but then I stop, remembering Rose. 'I can do this on my own,' I say. 'Will you find Rose and make sure she's safe? When the explosion happened I felt her being pulled out of my hands.'

Crowky nods. 'Fine, but you need to get rid of that fairy. You haven't got long.'

He turns towards the bed while I bundle Moss down the stairs. Rose and I might have taken away her magic, but we haven't taken away her ability to talk. As I carry her through the house and down into the cellar she shouts out a stream of insults.

'You are a silly, stupid, ugly, *smelly* boy, Arthur Trout! I should have got Owl to make a storm that sizzled you with lightning! I should have made Twig grow a tree round you that was so massive that it squished you and ATE YOU UP!'

I ignore all this as I carry her towards Grandad's jam cupboard. She twists inside the sari, but right now she's no stronger than a puppy. I kneel in front of the cupboard. Is Grandad's world really in there? Will the doorway work for me? If it doesn't, I'm in big trouble.

'I don't know where you think you're going to put me,' Moss snarls, as I open the doors, 'but wherever it is I'm going to smash it up, and then I'll escape and find you and then I'll . . . I'll . . .' She pauses as I push jam jars out of the way. I think she's run out of things to say. I stare at the boards at the back of the cupboard. If I'm going to find Grandad's world, I have to believe it's there.

Keeping a tight grip on Moss, I reach forward. 'You stinky, nasty boy!' she screams. 'Don't you *dare* put me in this cupboard!'

'It's not a cupboard,' I say. 'It's a doorway . . .' and then I try to remember every story Grandad has ever told me about his world. I picture his flying ship racing across a moonlit sky and I feel the star-spangled darkness wrap round me just like he said it had wrapped round him.

'Listen,' I tell Moss. 'Where you're going there's a sea witch, a *sorcière de la mer*. She has a terrible temper and silver fingernails. She eats sharks like they're fish fingers, and if you do *anything* bad she'll eat you too!'

'Ha!' Moss twists her head from side to side. 'I'd like to see her try!'

I ignore her and push my head inside the cupboard until my nose is almost touching the boards. Moss's cries of protest die away and I hear something else. Drifting from somewhere up ahead is the whisper of the wind, and the faint suck and splash of waves. A breeze brushes my face, blowing my hair, and I smell the tang of salt and seaweed. I reach my free hand forward. My fingers don't touch the back of the cupboard like they should. Instead they move into soft warm air.

I have an overwhelming urge to crawl, but just then Moss wriggles, trying to escape from under my arm, and I remember what I'm supposed to be doing.

'You'll be safe here,' I say. 'Just leave the witch alone.'

Then I loosen Nani's sari and push Moss forward. I feel a rush of sea air as she slips away from me and into the darkness at the back of the cupboard. 'Don't you DARE!' she screams, but gradually her voice fades away and then she's gone.

I blink and then all I can see behind Grandad's neatly labelled jars are solid planks of wood.

Slamming the doors shut I run for the stairs.

CHAPTER 56

I burst into the attic and see Rose lying on the floor. My relief that Crowky has found her lasts for a few blissful seconds, but then I realise something is wrong.

Rose is floppy and her eyes are half shut. Crowky is behind her, his hands squeezing her shoulders. He hasn't noticed me come in. His eyes are screwed shut with concentration. This is what he looked like when he brought the Crowgon to life.

I kneel next to Rose and grab her hand. It's cold. It's such a shock that for a moment a pain fills my chest and I forget to breathe. Rose is full of life and warmth. She's funny. She's fiery, loud and bossy. She's not this silent, lifeless person in front of me. This hand feels like it belongs to a stranger. I hold it against my warm face and Crowky presses down even harder on her shoulders.

'What are you feeling?' I manage to say.

'Not hate.' His voice is a harsh whisper. 'The other thing.'

'Me too,' I say, and I put my arms round Rose and cling

on to her muddy singed onesie. I hold her as close as I dare, as if I'm trying to share my heartbeat.

Then I feel it, faint and slow, but definitely there: another heartbeat. I stay like that until I see Rose's fingers moving.

I sit up. Rose's eyes flutter open. She doesn't see me, but she sees Crowky still gripping her shoulders. Smiling, she says, 'Crowky . . . Is that you?'

And then, for possibly the first time in his life, Crowky smiles too.

We stay like this, the three of us, sitting together, until Rose can sit up. She looks around the room, confused.

'What happened?' she says. 'Win mended my ankle with a spell – I'm not sure who was more surprised, him or me – and then we met Grandad up on the ledge. I came to find you and then there was this bang.'

'Moss opened the bed,' I say. 'Just a tiny bit and there was this explosion.'

'We need to go to Roar,' says Rose, trying to stand up. 'We need to make sure everyone is OK.'

We need to make sure we can still get there, I think, but I don't say this out loud. The thought is too frightening. It's obvious that Rose can't go anywhere yet so I say, 'I'll go,' and walk over to the camp bed. I kneel down. Just before I crawl inside I glance back and see the bizarre sight of Crowky helping Rose towards the sofa.

Quickly I push my head inside the mattress, then move forward, pulling in my shoulders and legs.

293

The mattress presses into my face. It smells of damp, and something else . . . *fireworks*, I think as I crawl further into the darkness. I keep moving, refusing to think about the explosion that knocked me away from the bed. Instead, I fill my mind with thoughts of Roar, of swaying trees and crashing waves, and when my hands touch cold stone I let out a breath I didn't realise I was holding.

Up ahead I see the leaves cover the end of the tunnel. They're not bright and golden like they usually are and for a moment I feel a pang of fear. Then I remember that it's night-time in Roar, just like it is in Home: there's no sunlight to shine on them. Instead a rainbow glow shimmers around the leaves. I focus on the shifting pinks and blues and greens as I crawl forward and push my face through the leaves.

Warm light falls over me and I see Roar lit up by the moon and stars. The river is a multicoloured ribbon that leads to the Bottomless Ocean. Wind brushes the tops of the dark trees. Roar is still here, perfect and beautiful.

I can hear voices. I peer over the ledge and see Win and Grandad sitting by the pool at the bottom of the waterfall. Win is holding something shiny in his hands. It's Grandad's penknife.

'Jay, are you sure this isn't a wand?' he says, then he gasps. 'It's got scissors! I want scissors on my wand!'

The happiness I feel is as warm as the stars above me and for a moment all I can do is smile and stare as Win thrusts the pen knife into the air shouting, 'Whistle fur!' followed by 'Mister Flambaygo!'

'Sorry, Jay,' he says passing back the pen knife. 'Your wand's broken.'

'Hey!' I shout, making them look up.

'Arthur!' cries Win. 'Mitch has put out the fires with a rain spell and I mended Rose's foot with some awesome magic, plus there's no Moss. It's brilliant!'

'Where is that fairy?' asks Grandad. 'Win here has told me that she's not quite as sweet as she seems.'

Quickly I tell Grandad that I've put Moss into his world. As I thought, he isn't angry at all. 'Best place for her,' he chuckles. 'I've got fairies too, only mine are big and they've got wings.'

A grumble coming from somewhere above my head tells me that the On-Off Waterfall is about to turn on.

'Jump down!' shouts Win. 'As soon as it's light I'm taking Jay to see the holes in the meadow. They're still full of water. We've got loads of swimming pools!'

'I've got to get Rose,' I say. 'I'll meet you at Mitch's.' I decide not to mention that right now Rose is lying flat out on Grandad's sofa and that Crowky is looking after her. If Grandad knows what just happened in his attic we might not get to spend our last day in Roar.

'I'd like to meet your mermaid friend,' Grandad says.

Win shakes his head. 'No you wouldn't, Jay. She's so sarcastic. She'll probably laugh at your beard.'

Just then water thunders down and I have to duck back behind the leaves. I turn and start to crawl back through the tunnel. Really I'd love to go off with Win and Grandad to see the meadow, but I can't, not yet. It's true that I have to get Rose, but there's something else I need to do.

CHAPTER 57

I never imagined that one day I would be sitting on the sofa in Grandad's attic drinking a cup of hot chocolate with Crowky.

Actually, it's Rose and me who are on the sofa. Crowky is on the beanbag. His knees are up near his sack face and his wings are scrunched up behind him. In one hand he holds a mug, in the other a chocolate digestive biscuit.

I'm trying not to stare, but it's really hard.

With every sip of hot chocolate, Rose looks better and better.

'Arthur, you didn't put in enough marshmallows,' she says, followed by, 'There's not enough chocolate powder either.'

'Sorry,' I say, smiling. Right now it's brilliant to be bossed around by Rose.

As she sips her drink, Rose flicks through her Fairy Fact File. 'So to take away the fairies' powers all we had to do was hold hands and say "Hear me roar"?' She waves her booklet in the air. 'I told you everything we needed to know about the fairies was in here.'

'You were right about the bed too,' I say. 'We can never open it.'

She rolls her eyes. 'Arthur, when are you going to learn? I'm right about everything!'

'You stopped the explosion.' Crowky's voice is a low whisper. 'I saw Moss open the bed and the flash of light, but it never got past you.'

'I saved Roar,' says Rose cheerfully. 'I'm a human lightning conductor!'

'And Crowky saved you,' I say.

Rose nods. 'I know. He's got amazing hands.'

Crowky scowls into his drink. He tosses his biscuit into his wide mouth then uses one twig finger from his 'amazing hands' to stir his hot chocolate. He hooks up a melting marshmallow and stares at it suspiciously.

'It's a marshmallow,' I say. 'They're nice. If you like them, Win can make you loads. Marshmallow-making is his best spell.'

Crowky shudders and lets the marshmallow plop back into his hot chocolate.

'I feel better,' says Rose, shrugging off the blanket. 'See.' She holds out her hands to show that they've stopped trembling. 'We should go back to Roar.'

'You go,' I say, 'and we'll follow. There's something I want to show Crowky.'

'OK,' she says, with a frown, 'but don't be too long. Remember, we've got one day left in Roar.'

'We can see the unicorns,' I say, 'and visit Boulders and Waterfalls!'

'And have a party,' says Rose. 'We need to celebrate getting rid of Moss.'

Then she gets off the sofa and kneels in front of the bed. Just before she sticks her head inside, she says, 'Thank you, Crowky. I'll never forget what you did for me.'

And then I see Crowky smile for a second time, but he quickly hides it behind his mug.

Rose crawls into the bed and seconds later she's gone.

'So,' I say to Crowky. 'Would you like to see Home?'

He looks up at me, blinks, then nods his heavy sack head.

CHAPTER 58

Obviously Crowky's wings are a problem, and his straw hair, and his sack face and twig fingers. But it's the middle of the night and I decide that if we stick to the shadows, no one will see us, and, worst-case scenario, if they do, Crowky can pick me up and we'll fly away. I get him to agree to all this before we leave the house.

First, we walk down Grandad's road, heading towards the seafront. Crowky is carrying Grandad's golf umbrella and it hides most of his face. Really it's only his wings poking out behind that give him away.

To begin with I talk, pointing out the things I think will interest him. 'Those are cars,' I say. 'People use them instead of bikes or flying. And those tall things are street lights, and that's a block of flats, lots of houses all stacked on top of each other.'

He glances at everything I point out, but when we reach the sea I realise he doesn't need my commentary. He's perfectly happy looking around.

I trail behind him as we walk along the prom, heading towards the pier. We wander through the empty bandstand and past closed cafés. He pauses by the still and silent merry-go-round, and jumps when a motorbike goes past.

He seems most interested in the coloured lights strung along the promenade, and the seagulls. We come across two seagulls devouring chips they've pulled out of a bin. They squabble over them and Crowky crouches down and stares at their curved orange beaks and yellow eyes.

When we reach the pier I notice that the sky is getting lighter. We'll need to turn back soon. We walk to the end of the pier, the dark sea sloshing below us, then stand and look back towards town.

We're tucked away in a dark corner. The arcade is behind us and I guess they don't turn everything off at night because inside lights flash and occasionally music blares out. The wind has swept yesterday's litter into a pile by our feet. Crowky nudges giant drink cups, fish and chip boxes and ketchup-smeared paper with the toe of his trainers.

'We should go,' I say. There are more gulls calling from the roof of the arcade. If the birds are waking up, then people will be next.

We walk back quickly. At one point we see a dog walker coming our way and we duck into one of the shelters that line the prom. The dog growls in our direction and the feathers on Crowky's wings puff up, but the owner is listening to

music and doesn't notice us hiding.

I only relax when we're walking down Grandad's driveway, which is hidden by trees. Once we're inside the house with the door firmly closed, I say, 'So that's Home. There's lots more of it – jungles, forests, cities. There's millions and millions more cars and houses and people. I only showed you a tiny bit of it.'

Crowky nods. It's hard to tell what he's thinking. His face is screwed up in his usual scowl.

'Look,' I say. 'You can stay if you want. I'm not going to try to stop you from doing things any more. I can't. I give up.'

He shakes his head and the straw inside him rustles. 'It's got too many lights and sounds, and not enough dragons. Roar is better.' Then he turns and stomps up the stairs, his wings brushing the walls.

CHAPTER 59

We find a note from Rose stuck to a tree at the bottom of the waterfall.

We've all gone to Mitch's island for breakfast. There's a dragon waiting in the meadow. The Lost Girls have taken their things out of the Crow's Nest. Crowky can go home or he can come to Mitch's if he likes.

I pass the note to Crowky and he reads it carefully. 'Do you want to come?' I say, trying and failing to imagine the moment when Crowky and I turn up to the breakfast party. 'Mitch makes amazing pancakes.'

Crowky shudders and I'm not sure if it's the thought of the pancakes or hanging out with us. 'I don't like sweet things,' he says.

'You don't have to eat the pancakes.'

He shakes his head stubbornly. 'I want to go home.'

'OK, but before you go, I want to give you something.' I pass Crowky the knight from Grandad's chess set. I picked it up on our way through the attic.

He holds it between two fingers and looks at it suspiciously. 'It's the unicorn from I'm Coming to Get You,' he says. 'Why would I want this? It's not even got a horn!'

'It's more than that,' I say. 'It's a key to Home. If you ever need us, or want to see us, just crawl into the tunnel holding it and you'll end up in Grandad's attic. It's a thank-you for saving Rose.'

He stares at the chess piece then says, 'But I've tried to hurt her hundreds of times . . .'

'I know, but you never did, did you? And today you saved her.'

After a moment he nods and slips the chess piece in his pocket. Then he stares at the ground.

'Right, well, I suppose I'd better get going,' I say.

I start to walk away then Crowky calls after me. 'Arthur, next time you come to Roar, visit the Crow's Nest. We'll play I'm Coming to Get You. Bring Rose . . . I can beat her too.' Before I can reply he snaps open his wings and half flying, half running, he disappears into the shadows of the forest.

I walk towards the meadow. Smoke from my waiting dragon drifts towards me and all around me insects hum. As I walk, I think about how strange it is to be invited to play chess at the Crow's Nest. Strange, but definitely good.

It's Vlad who takes me to Mitch's island. My landing is perfect, probably because I leave him to it. Feeling utterly exhausted, but totally happy, I half fall off his back then crunch my way over shells and sand towards Mitch's hut.

I hear a ukulele playing and laughter, and, when I push aside a sunflower, I see everyone gathered there.

Grandad is lying in Mitch's hammock, eyes closed, a mug of pink resting on his stomach. Rose and Mitch are sitting at the end of the jetty. It's actually Rose who's playing the ukulele. Mitch is leaning back and flicking her tail through the water in time to the music. The Lost Girls are swimming. Well, swimming and fighting. Stella isn't. She's standing on the deck, hands on hips, watching over them like a lifeguard.

'I said, NO biting!' she yells. 'I saw that, Sophie!'

'I'm playing fairies!' shouts Sophie.

'Well don't!' replies Stella.

Talking of biting, Twig, Pebble and Owl are helping Win to make a magical bonfire. Actually, Twig and Owl are, and Pebble is watching, along with some birds, a snail and a small cloud of butterflies. Twig is wriggling his fingers, making a pile of wood grow bigger and Win has conjured up Mister Flambaygo and is attempting to roll the ball of fire towards the wood. Owl has made a breeze that is fanning the flames. The ball of fire grows bigger and bigger.

'Oooh, ow!' Win cries, blowing on his fingers. 'Bit less wind, Owl.'

But Owl seems so happy to be playing bonfires with Win – and possibly to be free of Moss – that he sends out a massive gust of wind that wafts Mister Flambaygo straight over the bonfire and into the lagoon. It disappears under the water with a loud hiss.

'Nice,' says Win, giving Owl a pat on the shoulder. 'You just heated the lagoon *and* made waves!'

He's right. The wind flowing from Owl's fingers has made waves ripple across the surface of the lagoon, getting bigger as they go. The Lost Girls love it. They start screaming and letting themselves be rolled up and down. Win sighs happily. 'Together our magic is *imaginary*!'

The fairies jump into the lagoon with the Lost Girls, but Win stays where he is. He's staring at something, mesmerised. I push aside the sunflower and go and join him.

'Arthur!' he says when he sees me. 'Look!'

He's taken Rose's dragon's egg out of its bag and is cradling it in his hands. It trembles and a tiny hole appears in the shell. A glittering yellow eye peers out of the hole, blinks, then disappears. Next a thin trail of smoke seeps out.

'Rose!' Win shouts. 'Come quick! Your egg is hatching!'

His words bring everyone rushing over. Grandad struggles out of the hammock and the Lost Girls pull themselves, dripping, from the lagoon.

By the time Rose reaches us the dragon has stuck its head out of the egg and is gazing at Win. Its scales are bright green and its wings are as thin as tissue paper.

'Hobellobo!' says Rose reaching a finger towards the dragon. The dragon whips its head round and puffs a miniature ball of fire in her direction.

'*Ow!*' she says, jumping back. Then she laughs. 'I don't believe it. I kept that egg safe for days and then it goes and hatches for Win!'

'What do you mean?' he says, his eyes wide.

'Well, it saw you first, didn't it? A dragon belongs to the first person it sees, which, annoyingly, Win, was you.'

Win gasps and strokes the dragon's twisting neck. The little creature wraps its tail round his finger and stares up at him. 'So this is *my* dragon?' he says.

Rose smiles and shrugs. 'I suppose it's only fair. I have got three already.'

'I've got a dragon! I'VE GOT A FLIPPING DRAGON!' cries Win, then he holds it aloft and adds, 'And its name shall be . . . *Arthur!*'

CHAPTER 60

'Arthur, keep going!' Rose shoves me from behind, but I can't crawl any faster because Grandad is blocking my way.

'It's fascinating,' he says. 'One of my hands is on stone, and the other one is on mattress. I'm exactly halfway between Roar and Home!'

'That's great, Grandad,' I say, 'but I'm stuck between you and Rose right now and I could do with some fresh air.'

'Righto!' he says, and he carries on crawling towards the light.

We pull ourselves out of the folding camp bed, then flop down on the attic floor. We've spent the whole day in Roar. Grandad barely moved from Mitch's hammock – which he claims is the best place in Roar – but Rose and I crammed in as much as we possibly could.

We went with Stella and the Lost Girls to visit Treetops, and it was amazing. They've rebuilt loads of it and even added some extra features inspired by their stay in the

Crow's Nest. There are spiral staircases made out of twisting branches – Twig has promised to help improve these – and each girl has her own nest to sleep in.

'Once you've slept in a nest, you can't go back,' Stella explained.

Then Rose rode off on Prosecco to meet up with Mitch, and Win and I went to find our unicorns. We spent the rest of the day trotting around Roar on Ronaldo and Penguin. If we saw a pool, we swam in it. If we found a tempting vine, we swung on it.

Arthur the baby dragon was with us the whole time, usually snuggled up in Penguin's mane. I tried to persuade Win that having a dragon called Arthur might get confusing, especially as she's a girl dragon, but he said this way he gets to have an Arthur with him all the time.

He also told me that he's invited Twig, Owl and Pebble to stay at his cave until they find a place of their own to live. 'You don't mind do you, Arthur?' he'd asked.

I told him that I thought it was a brilliant idea. Moss might have been wicked, but she was their big sister and told them what to do, so for a while he's going to have to be their big brother and look after them. When I left he was full of his plans to establish a magical ninja-fairy-wizard training academy at his cave, with Owl, Twig and Pebble as his first students.

Back in the attic, Grandad yawns dramatically then gets to his feet. 'Well, I don't know about you two, but I think a bit of food is in order, then a bath and an early night. Your mum and dad will be back first thing in the morning and if you look like you do right now, they'll never let you stay with me again.'

He walks towards the door. 'Hang on, Grandad,' I say, and I pick up his 'NO PROB-LLAMA!' T-shirt from the floor. 'Do you want this back?'

'My T-shirt!' he says happily, and he takes it and wanders down the stairs, muttering about how it will be 'as good as new' after a wash.

'I want the first bath,' I say, getting up to follow him.

'Hang on a minute, Arthur,' says Rose. 'There's something we need to do.'

'What?'

'Play.'

I stare at her. 'Play? Really, Rose? We spent last night fighting a fairy who tried to destroy Roar, and the night before that you had your skin stolen and I was trapped in a cave with Crowky. I don't know about you, but I could do with a bit of sleep right now.'

'It's important,' she insists.

'What could possibly be more important than sleep?'

I couldn't have predicted her next words. 'We need to make a friend for Crowky,' she says. 'Someone good at chess and strong enough to stand up to him. He's got Pebble, but she's got her brothers, and you've got Win and I've got Mitch. Crowky needs someone of his own.'

I realise that she's right. We've already agreed that the next time we visit Roar we'll go to the Crow's Nest. We know Pebble will see him, but what about the rest of the time? Crowky will be lonely in his castle, but we can change that.

'It needs to be someone who can keep his mind busy,' I say, 'and distract him from dastardly thoughts, and funny would be good too. He could definitely do with learning how to laugh.'

Rose thinks for moment then looks up at me and grins. 'I've got it!' she says. 'Just give me a minute.'

She runs to the trunk where Grandad keeps our old toys and starts to rummage through it. She finds a bag of dressing-up clothes and disappears behind the sofa. 'Nearly ready!' she calls.

After a couple of minutes she stands up. She's got her back to me and her arms outstretched and she's wearing a curly blonde wig on her head that I'm fairly certain she last wore when she was pretending to be Candyfloss. She makes her fingers stiff and lets her head flop down. She's pretending to be a scarecrow. It's actually pretty scary.

Suddenly she swings round, then her head pings up. 'Hello, Arthur Trout!' Her voice is like a rusty nail being pulled down a blackboard.

Even though I know it's just Rose wearing a wig and a strange assortment of dressing-up clothes I still feel a little shiver of fear. 'Who are you?' I say.

'Merla McCraw!'

I swallow. 'And . . . do you want to *get me* by any chance?'

Rose, no, *Merla McCraw* rolls her eyes. 'No! I've got better things to do than waste my time on you, Arthur Trout!'

Then for the next half-hour Merla McCraw and I play in the attic.

Except at some point I stop being me, Arthur Trout, and I become Crowky. Merla and I find the Crowgon at the bottom of the muddy pit in the meadow and we get it working again – it turns out Merla's hands are excellent at giving life. She finds the opposite of hate much easier than Crowky.

We fly around Roar on the Crowgon and scare the Lost Girls, but just a bit, then we go back to the Crow's Nest where, after a quick tour, we sit on the balcony playing I'm

Coming to Get You. We make plans to invite the fairies over and wonder if they might like to build some tree houses inside the castle. 'They could stay if they wanted,' says Merla. 'There's plenty of room.'

'Do you mind that there's not much sun here?' I ask.

'No,' Merla snaps. 'I hate the sun.'

At one point Merla gets angry because Crowky wins and she tips the entire I'm Coming to Get You board over the side of the balcony, but Crowky doesn't mind. He understands. Plus now they can make a new board together with moving, living pieces.

Merla is getting ready to dive off the edge of the balcony (the back of the sofa) to test her wings when she yawns and pulls off her wig.

And, just like that, I'm back in the attic with my sister, and the game is over.

'I'm hungry,' Rose says. 'Let's ask Grandad if we can get fish and chips.'

Before we go, we push the folding camp bed into the corner and cover it with Nani's sari. Tomorrow, before Mum and Dad arrive, we're going to get a rope and wind it round and round the bed and tie it with so many knots that it's impossible to open. Grandad's got a plan to make a 'camp bed non-opening device' involving welding together some golf clubs, but the rope will have to do for now.

'Come on,' says Rose, heading towards the door. 'If we don't hurry, the chip shop will be closed.'

But I can't quite bring myself to turn away from the bed and leave Roar behind.

'It will be half-term soon,' says Rose. 'We can visit Roar then.'

She always knows what I'm thinking. I force myself to leave the attic and the camp bed behind and I follow her down the stairs.

'Rose, do you think it worked?' I say. 'Next time we go to Roar, will Merla be there?'

Rose looks back and smiles. 'It worked. I can feel it. That was a good game, Arthur.'

'It was better than good,' I say. 'It was imaginary.'

'Totally,' she says, and then we run downstairs to find Grandad and demand our fish and chips.

ACKNOWLEDGEMENTS

I could not have written the Land of Roar trilogy without the help and advice of many kind and talented people.

I would like to thank the team at Farshore – previously Egmont Books – who championed Roar from the very beginning: Laura Bird, Olivia Carson, Siobhan McDermott and Hilary Bell, thank you for everything you have done and do to make the Land of Roar spring into life. A huge thank you to Ali Dougal for seeing what Roar could become – you made my dreams come true. Thank you to Liz Bankes, editor extraordinaire, creator of the magic road, Mitch's tail and champion of Carol Brocklebank; and thank you to Lindsey Heaven for picking up the Roar baton and becoming the second mother of dragons.

Thank you to my writing pals in Brighton and my writing pal in Eastbourne. How many bowls of soup at Helen Dennis's house does it take to write a fantasy trilogy? Around one hundred.

A special thanks goes to Ben Mantle for creating the most beautiful artwork for the Land of Roar. In my wildest dreams I never imagined my words could come to life in such a magical way.

Thank you to my patient and lovely family – Mum, Dad, Ben, Nell and Flora – who followed Roar every step of the way and gave me time, encouragement, inspiration, confidence and lots of spells. Thank you to my brother, Nick, my sister, Julia, and our cousins – our games were the best.

Finally, two thank yous that are as vast as Bottomless Ocean.

Thank you (again) to my husband, Ben, for giving me the initial idea and helping me create most of the Land of Roar on one long, windy walk over the cliffs. Crowky, Prosecco, Win, Mitch and the Lost Girls all came to life that day. There would be no Land of Roar without you.

And thank you to my agent, Julia Churchill, who, after patiently listening to my latest ideas, told me to write *The Land of Roar*. As usual, she was right. Thanks, Julia, you're imaginary.

AUTHOR Q&A

What first sparked the idea for *The Land of Roar?*

When I was little I used to play in the attic of my nan's house with my brother, sister and cousins. There was a camp bed up there (very like the one in the books) and we would dare each other to crawl through the middle of the folded mattress. I remember feeling a thrilling combination of fear and excitement as I stuck my head into that mattress. I would have loved to discover the Land of Roar on the other side, but unfortunately I always ended up back in my nan's attic. When I wrote *The Land of Roar* I was making a dream come true for eight-year-old me.

If you could spend a day in Roar, what would you do?

I'd have breakfast at Win's cave (toast, obviously) then I'd set off on Prosecco to visit Boulders and Waterfalls. This area of Roar is basically a giant waterpark and I based it on the pools I swam in when I visited the Northern Territory in Australia. Lunch would be a picnic with the Lost Girls at Treetops (bees on toast), then I'd catch a dragon and fly to Mitch's island to swim in the lagoon under the rainbow stars. If I was feeling daring I might pop to the Crow's Nest to see Crowky. We'd play I'm Coming to Get You and maybe I'd slide all the way down the giant twisting staircase. One of the best things about writing is that my real memories get confused with Arthur Trout's memories. I can imagine all this happening very easily!

If you could make your own fantasy world, what would be in it and what would it be called?

The Land of Roar is my own fantasy world, and I wouldn't change a thing except the name. I'd have to call it the Land of Jen. Oh, and I'd add some baths, toothbrushes and toothpaste.

What is your favourite thing about being a writer?

The fact that when I write I feel like the things I'm describing are happening to me. It's the best magic trick in the world. I've flown dragons and been chased through the snow by wolves. I've wandered barefoot on the deck of the *Alisha* and shared pic 'n' mix with orangutans. I felt Crowky's stick fingers grabbing hold of me and I've camped out on deserted islands. The only limit on where I can go and what I can do is my imagination.

What is your top tip for a writer starting their story ?

I don't start writing a story until it is alive in my head. I spend much more time thinking about a story than I do actually writing it. I make up the settings, put my characters in these settings and get them talking to each other. I play with the plot. I draw pictures and plans. I daydream like this for hours until my story feels real. Then, when I start writing, I don't feel like I'm making anything up; I feel like I'm describing something that's actually happened to me. So my top tip is: daydream and play for as long as you possibly can.

Believing is just the beginning . . .